THE 3 INVESTIGATORS

"WE INVESTIGATE ANYTHING"

Jupiter Jones, Founder

Pete Crenshaw, Associate   Bob Andrews, Associate

Jupe is the brain. Pete is the jock. And Bob is Mr. Cool. Together they can solve just about any crime in Rocky Beach, California.

But can they solve a theft at a comic-book convention—when a comic-book character commits the crime?

This kind of funny business is *not* funny!

THE THREE INVESTIGATORS
C R I M E B U S T E R S

THE 3 INVESTIGATORS

CRIMEBUSTERS™ #4

Funny Business

by
WILLIAM McCAY

based on characters created by Robert Arthur

Borzoi Sprinters
ALFRED A. KNOPF · NEW YORK

DR. M. JERRY WEISS, Distinguished Service Professor of Communications at Jersey City State College, is the educational consultant for Borzoi Sprinters. A past chair of the International Reading Association President's Advisory Committee on Intellectual Freedom, he travels frequently to give workshops on the use of trade books in schools.

Library of Congress Cataloging-in-Publication Data
McCay, William.
Funny business / by William McCay ;
based on characters created by Robert Arthur.
p.   cm.—(The 3 investigators. Crimebusters ; #4)
Summary: The Three Investigators track a costumed thief at a comic-book convention.
ISBN 0-394-89981-4 (pbk.)
[1. Cartoons and comics—Collectors and collecting—Fiction.
2. Mystery and detective stories]   I. Arthur, Robert.   II. Title.
III. Series: 3 investigators. Crimebusters ; #4.
PZ7.M4784136Fu   1989b   [Fic]—dc19   88-45879

RL: 6.0
Also available in a library edition from Random House, Inc.—
ISBN 0-394-99981-9

Manufactured in the United States of America
10   9   8   7   6   5   4   3   2   1

1

Comix!

"WHAT THE. . . ?" JUPITER JONES LOOKED UP FROM THE car engine he was supposed to be working on. He straightened quickly, nearly cracking his head on the hood of the old white Chevy Impala. As the founder of The Three Investigators, Jupe was a keen, cool-headed observer. But even a 17-year-old detective can be left gawking sometimes.

Uncle Titus had just returned from a collecting trip. Titus Jones was famous for coming up with the world's strangest salvage. His finds dotted the grounds of The Jones Salvage Yard. From the auto grease pit Jupe could see some of them—the herd of carousel horses, the clump of candy-striped barber poles. But from the look of things, this time Uncle Titus had outdone himself.

Sitting behind the wheel of the yard's large collection truck, Jupe's uncle wore a fur cap with a raccoon tail down the back. In the back of the pickup Hans and Konrad were trying out hula hoops.

Jupe brushed back his dark brown hair, his eyes

wide with disbelief at the spectacle. As he eased his stocky frame around the Impala's hood to see what his aunt would make of all this his elbow struck a can of motor oil. It began glugging its contents into the crankcase.

"Oof!" A thump came from under the chassis. Jupe's pal Pete Crenshaw shot out from below the car. "You're not supposed to pour until I put the plug back in!"

Pete was a tall, athletic guy, one of Jupe's associates in The Three Investigators detective agency. He didn't look his best lying on a wheeled mechanic's board, sputtering from a mouthful of fresh oil. The stuff had also plastered down his reddish-brown hair.

The idea had been to drain the old oil out of Pete's latest used car and put some new lubricant into the engine. But that was before Jupe's oil spill.

Jupe grabbed for the now empty can. "Sorry," he apologized. "I got—distracted."

"By what? World War III?" Then Pete caught sight of Jupe's Aunt Mathilda. The tall, heavyset woman was marching toward the truck. "Uh-oh. Maybe that's exactly what it will be."

"Titus Jones," Aunt Mathilda burst out. "Where did you find this, this"—she waved her arms helplessly—"this *junk*?"

"It isn't junk," Uncle Titus protested. "It's prime salvage material. Collector's items."

"Like that silly hat on your head?"

Uncle Titus flicked the fur tail. "It's a genuine Davy Crockett coonskin cap."

Aunt Mathilda quickly walked to the back of the truck. "Collector's items, my foot. Hula hoops. Pogo sticks. And what's in this trunk?" She flipped up the heavy top and sucked in her breath. "Comic books! You actually spent money for this?"

Although Jupe was overweight, he could move fast when he wanted to. Now he hurried over to the pickup for a look. Inside the trunk, just as his aunt had said, were mounds and mounds of comics.

"Wow!" Pete muttered beside him. "This guy must have really loved comics."

"They look pretty old," Jupe said. "Those books must have been tucked away for years." He turned to Pete. "How much money do you have on you?"

"Not a lot." Pete began digging through his pockets.

"Hey, guys, what's up?" Bob Andrews asked, grinning. The tall, blond third Investigator had just walked in through the salvage yard gate. He looked tanned and trim in a white polo shirt and pleated khaki pants. Jupe was almost surprised to find him alone. Ever since Bob had replaced his glasses with contact lenses, a fan club of girls could be expected to be tagging after him—if they weren't hanging around the junkyard waiting for him to show up.

Now Jupe pounced on him. "How much money have you got?"

Bob reached into his pocket. "You're catching me at a bad time. What do you need it for?"

Jupe grinned. "I want to buy some comics."

Up on the truck Aunt Mathilda was still poking

through the contents of the trunk. "They may be valuable. But how do we find out? And where will we find buyers?"

"Right here." Jupe snatched the money from Bob and Pete, adding it to the bills he'd found in his own pockets. "I have . . ." He counted quickly. "Twenty-one dollars and seventeen cents. We'll undertake all the worry and work. How about it, Aunt M?"

"Done!" Aunt Mathilda grabbed the money. Uncle Titus looked as if he were about to argue. Then he saw the look in his wife's eyes.

But Jupe got a lot of argument from his friends as they unloaded the trunk.

"You borrowed our money to buy *this*?" Bob grunted as they swung the big box down.

"Jupe's losing it," Pete said. "First he pours motor oil all over my face and now he pulls this."

"Motor oil, huh?" Bob leaned toward Pete's head and sniffed. "I thought you were using some new kind of hair-styling stuff."

"If you two have finished clowning around," Jupe said, "I'll explain about your brilliant investment."

"*Our* investment?" Bob asked, frowning.

"You'll see your money several times over." Jupe tapped the trunk. "Depending on what we find inside."

"That junk?" Pete's voice was disbelieving.

"Buried treasure," Jupe insisted. "Do you know what some of those old comics go for? Some are worth thousands of dollars."

"*Thousands* . . . ?" Bob stared at the trunk.

"Of course, we don't know what's in there," Jupe went on. "We may find only a few hundred dollars' worth." He rubbed his hands together. "My hope is that the proceeds will be enough for me to buy a car. Whatever there is, we'll divide it three ways. Agreed?"

♦ ♦ ♦

The next Friday afternoon the Investigators were in Pete's Impala, heading toward downtown Los Angeles. For once, all three guys had the weekend free. Pete's girlfriend, Kelly Madigan, had gone away to cheerleaders' camp. Bob had a few days off from his part-time job at Sax Sendler's Rock-Plus talent agency. And Jupe could call his time his own now that he'd computerized the junkyard inventory for Aunt Mathilda.

Pete glared in the rear-view mirror at the trail of smoke the Impala left behind. "You know, Jupe, we're still burning oil from that can you spilled all over the engine," he grumbled. "And I swear I can still smell that gunk on my hair."

"At least you're not half-blind from going through all those stupid comics," Bob said. "Sorting out those books while Jupe figured out how much they were worth was worse than my old library job."

"I think having all those comics is kind of neat," said Pete. "You know, I remember reading some of them when I was a little kid. The Crimson Phantom . . ." He shook his head and sighed. "He was my all-time favorite."

"You can afford to be nostalgic," Bob complained. "You were out with Kelly most of the time we were working. Jupe's too chicken to try interrupting *her* social life." Kelly Madigan had not only efficiently staked out Pete as her boyfriend—she'd just as firmly staked out most of his spare time as well.

In the back, Bob shot a dirty look at the cardboard box on the floor. "So I got stuck digging through this junk." He gave the box of comics a kick.

"Careful," Jupe said, turning in his seat. "You don't want to damage the merchandise. What we have here is the *crème de la crème* of the books we sorted out—the most valuable ones. But they have to be in mint condition if we expect to sell them at the InterComiCon."

"We'd *better* unload them," said Bob. "I want my money back! Lucky you read that article about the comics convention in the paper."

Jupiter grinned. "Bob, I'll put you in charge of counting the money afterward. Maybe that will improve your mood."

"We're here," Pete announced. "The Century Grand Plaza."

Bob stared at the glass and steel tower shining against the clear sky. "Pretty ritzy place to sell comics."

"It's August and sweltering," Jupe pointed out. "I'm sure they're happy to get any convention. Shall we park and find the action?"

They drove down a driveway into the hotel's underground parking garage. It looked like a weird concrete forest, with thick round pillars holding up the ceiling—and the building above them. The hotel management had tried to dress up the area with a bright coat of paint. But car exhaust and the shadows cast by all those pillars left the garage looking pretty dingy.

Pete pulled into an empty space. "Last stop. Everybody out."

"We've got a job for some muscles here," Bob said, dragging out the cardboard box of comics.

"Give me a break. I just drove you guys over here!" Pete protested.

"*I* could have driven," Bob said.

"We wouldn't have fit in your VW bug," Pete told him. "Not with Jupe—*and* that box of comic books."

Jupe glared at both of his friends. "*I'll* carry the comics." He grabbed the box. "I've got muscles too, you know. Judo class keeps me in shape."

"You'd be in better shape if you studied karate, like Bob and me," Pete said.

"Not true," puffed Jupe as he headed for the elevator.

The elevator opened as soon as Bob hit the call button.

As the doors closed, however, the guys heard the quick slap of footfalls. Someone was running to catch the elevator. An arm shot through the narrowing space to catch the doors before they shut. The doors sprang open—to reveal a man whose flesh was melting off his body!

2

Let's Make a Deal

THE BOX OF COMICS DROPPED FROM JUPE'S ARMS AS THE horrifying creature leaped into the elevator.

"Hey, sorry." The melting man caught the box in midair. He turned to the Investigators, who shrank away from him. "What's the problem?" he asked, then grinned as he realized the answer. "Oh, my costume!"

He flicked one of the gross-looking folds of flesh dripping off his shoulder. "Latex. I'm dressed as the Outrageous Ooze for the big costume contest. What do you think?"

"V-very realistic," Jupe managed to say.

The elevator reached the lobby, and with a "Got to run!" the Outrageous Ooze disappeared into the crowd. Others in the lobby were dressed as comic-strip characters, too. The Investigators crossed marble tiles and thick carpets to the chrome-framed announcement board. "InterComiCon—main conference hall," Jupe read. "This must be pretty big."

They headed for the conference area and found a line stretching in front of a plain wooden table.

Behind the table sat a girl with dyed blond hair and four-inch dark roots, wearing a black T-shirt with INTERCOMICON STAFF in white letters. "Ten dollars each," she said as the Investigators reached her. She took their money, thumped a stamp on a large black ink pad, and imprinted something on the backs of their right hands.

Jupe noticed that the girl with two-toned hair seemed to hold on to Bob's hand a little longer than necessary. For the first time she smiled.

Pete noticed, too. "If he could bottle whatever makes girls act that way . . ."

Jupe sighed. "I'd buy a case." He studied the stamp mark on his hand. INTERCOMICON—DAY 1. "Cheaper than tickets—smarter too." He glanced at Pete. "We can't go back out and give the stamp to a friend."

They followed Bob to the doorway of the conference hall. But a big guy in another staff T-shirt blocked the way. He checked their stamps, gave them a smile that displayed a chipped tooth, then moved aside. Pete, Bob, and Jupe stepped forward—into sheer craziness.

After the quietly expensive lobby, the scene inside looked like a rug traders' bazaar. The vast open space was broken up by hundreds of folding wooden tables, all arranged in squares to form makeshift stalls. Some tables served as counters, piled high with comics. At the back of each stall rose shelves and display boards, made colorful by comics displayed with their covers out. Carefully wrapped in protective plastic, these comics were obviously serious collector's items.

But even more numerous than the stalls were the people crammed into the aisles between them. Kids and adults pored over stacks of comics, made deals with the people behind the counters, or just tried to push their way through the crowd. Costumed characters showed themselves off. The noise was deafening.

As the three friends stood frozen in the doorway, a tall, thin red-haired man in an InterComiCon T-shirt detached himself from the chaos. He grinned at Jupe, Bob, and Pete.

"First-timers," he said. "I can tell from the stunned look. Welcome to the InterComiCon. I'm Axel Griswold. Supposedly I'm in charge of this madhouse." He glanced at the box in Jupe's arms. "What brings you here, guys?"

After hearing their story, his grin got bigger. "Well, there are lots of dealers," he said, spreading his arms. "But the biggest in the show is a bunch called Kamikaze Komics. They've got the money to give you the best deal. Check 'em out—their stall's over there." He pointed a long, elegant finger at one side of the room.

Following Griswold's instructions, the guys set off into the crowd. Jupe slowed them down for a moment when he stopped at a small stand that sold T-shirts as well as comics. He got each of them a red shirt printed with the message COMIC LOVERS DO IT WITH PICTURES. Working their way deep into the room, the Investigators found the Kamikaze Komics stall. It had a great location—half a wall on the right side, lots of products on sale—and lots of customers. The guys paused before approaching the tables. They wanted to spy out this operation.

Five young guys stood behind the tables, dealing with various customers. One, wearing a single earring, was selling a comic to a young kid. "There you go, *Thunderbeam* Number Three, only four dollars." He held out the comic, whose cover showed a hero blasting a hole through a tank with laser beams from his eyes. "You're lucky, kid. I doubt you'd be able to find this anywhere else in the show."

The kid eagerly handed over his money.

Bob muttered to his friends, "On the way over here I saw that same comic in the one-dollar pile at another dealer's stall."

Pete shook his head. "I remember buying it when it was new—and it only cost fifty cents."

As the Investigators came closer to the Kamikaze stall they saw a TV hooked up to a VCR. A salesman with bleached spiky hair and a black T-shirt was showing a scene from *Astro-Aces*, the hot new sci-fi TV show. "The syndicators send out the new episodes a week in advance. We intercept the satellite beam, tape the show, and you can have it before anybody else in town."

He grinned in triumph as his customer, a guy in his late twenties, eagerly came up with bills.

"He's paying for something he could see for nothing in a few days," Pete whispered.

"And paying for a pirated tape," Bob added.

"I see that 'be the first on your block' is still a strong selling strategy," Jupe murmured, hoisting his box of comics.

A salesman glanced over at them. "Can I help you guys?" The Investigators hesitated. "Hey, if you're not dealing, you're blocking people who will."

"No," Jupe said. "I don't think we're dealing."

As they headed away from the stall he turned to Bob. "Where did you see that other comic? The one without the grotesque price?"

"Back this way," Bob answered. "Near the emergency exit. It was a stall with a crazy name—nutcase or something."

The stall had a madman in its name, not a nutcase—Madman Dan's Comix Emporium. And the man behind the table fit the part perfectly with his wild curly black hair and bushy mustache. "Marty, head upstairs and get some more comic boxes," he said to a young guy, obviously his assistant. Then he turned to a gloomy-looking tall man with a fringe of graying hair around his bald dome. "Back again?"

"Three hundred fifty for that copy of *Fan Fun*," the man offered the dealer.

Madman Dan simply shook his head. "Five."

The man looked gloomier, but tried to bargain. "Four fifty."

"Six."

A note of desperation crept into the buyer's voice. "But the marked price is only four fifty."

"Now it's six," the wild-looking dealer replied.

·The man clenched his fists. "All right, six hundred dollars."

Madman Dan's smile got larger. "You waited too long. The price is now seven."

The man's jaw dropped. "Seven hundred! Don't you want anyone to buy it?"

"Close," said Madman Dan. "I don't want *you* to buy it."

The bald man turned on his heel and stormed off. Jupe watched him go. "Do you always treat your customers like that?" he asked.

"Only when they're creeps," Madman Dan replied. "That guy works for one of the major comic publishers. He's also a major creep. Now," he said, looking at the Investigators' box. "Are you here to buy or to deal?"

"We're here to sell," Jupe said, opening the carton.

The dealer checked out the contents. "Some interesting stuff," he said, eyes gleaming. "A couple of Silver Age books in good condition, a lot of fairly recent Number Ones. . . . Tell you what—four hundred for the whole package."

Jupe could feel the color rising in his face. "Only four? That's half what these are worth. I checked out the prices—"

"In the *Overstreet Guide*," Madman Dan finished. "They say you should be getting a lot more, right? But did you read the fine print at the beginning of *Overstreet*? The part where they explain that what they list are averages, and that prices differ from place to place? Not to mention that there's a little thing called profit."

"Profit, not rob—" Jupe said before Bob and Pete managed to pull him out of earshot.

"Don't kill the deal," they warned. "We're making a lot on our twenty bucks."

"We'll make more," Jupe promised them. "It's just a matter of bargaining. . . ."

He turned to face Madman Dan, but his eyes never made it to the dealer. They were snagged by a vision in blue and gold.

It was a tall girl about their age. Glorious blond hair swept nearly to her waist and shone against a blue silky cape. The rest of her outfit looked like a skimpy bathing suit made from glistening gold cloth. It showed off her deeply tanned arms and legs perfectly. As she walked along in her matching gold boots, she was simply breathtaking.

Madman Dan followed Jupe's gaze and grinned. "Eye-catching, huh? She's dressed as Stellara Stargirl for the costume contest. *Her* kind of costume I can understand. So why does someone covered in green slime always win?"

"Um, yes. Now, about these books . . ." But Jupe couldn't take his eyes off the girl.

"Look—" Madman Dan riffled through the box in Jupe's arms and pulled out ten comics. "These titles I can really sell. Can we make a partial deal? Let's say . . . three hundred just for these guys."

Jupe wasn't listening.

"The man made you an offer, Jupe," Bob whispered in his ear.

Jupe tore his gaze back to the comic books. "That begins to sound fairer." His head began turning again, toward the golden girl.

He caught a glimpse, but she disappeared behind a costumed figure all in red. The costume looked like a monk's robe—except for the searing color. As the figure came closer Jupe saw that its face was covered with a black-and-white skull mask.

Jupe shook his head and turned back to Madman Dan. He was all business again. "Right. Three hundred. Those are our most valuable comics, and I suspect you're still doing too well on the deal—"

The costumed character brushed past him, the red robe billowing out. Jupe turned in annoyance.

He saw the figure throw up its arms in a dramatic gesture. Long fingers stretched out, the pale white backs of the hands tightening. Four little balls fell to the floor. Then Madman Dan's whole stall disappeared in smoke!

3

Burned!

THE SUDDEN SMOKE CLOUD CAUSED SOME SHOUTING AND screaming among frightened comic buyers. But that was nothing compared with the screaming that started when the smoke began to clear.

"I've been robbed!" Madman Dan yelled at the top of his lungs. His mop of black curls was wilder than ever, and his mustache bristled. "Where's the guy in the Crimson Phantom costume? I'll kill him!"

Of course, the figure in the red robe had disappeared.

"Pretty slick," Jupe said. "He made his own smoke screen, then vaulted over the table to steal the valuable comics."

He stared at the wooden display board behind the stand, where a big hole had appeared among the comics. Madman Dan was staring, too. "He got my copy of *Fan Fun* Number One . . ."

The same comic that the bald man was bargaining for—and couldn't get, Jupe thought.

". . . And a bunch of twenty- and thirty-dollar

books." The dealer's voice was puzzled, and Jupe soon saw why. Three rows over and two up was a copy of *Flash* Number One—with a price tag of $4,500.

"Maybe the smoke wasn't such a good idea," Jupe suggested. "The thief may have missed what he was really aiming for."

"He did enough damage," Madman Dan said. "Plus on the way across the table he grabbed the books in my hand—*your* comics."

The Investigators stared at one another. The costumed Crimson Phantom had made off with their ten best books—and done them out of at least three hundred bucks!

"Looks like we've got a case to solve," Pete said.

"Case? Solve?" The dealer gave them a sharp look.

"That's what we do," Jupe explained. "Maybe you noticed these were tucked inside our comics." He held out one of their business cards.

"The Three Investigators?" Madman Dan said. "Hey, wait a second." He reached under the table and came out with a small box. Rummaging through, he pulled out a dog-eared card.

"I don't believe it!" said Bob. "He's got one of our old cards."

"Sure," said Madman Dan. "The card with the question marks. It goes for a buck seventy-five."

Jupe blinked. "You mean you're selling this?"

Madman Dan shrugged. "Some people will collect anything." He looked at them for a long moment. "So, you guys solve mysteries. Well, you're just what I need right now. Tell you what. Recover my comics as well as yours, and I'll give you exactly what *Overstreet* says yours are worth."

The Investigators looked at one another. "You've got a deal," Jupe said. He picked up the box of leftover comics and stuck out his free hand.

"Fine. I'm Dan DeMento." The dealer smiled under his shaggy mustache. "With a name like that you can see why people call me Madman."

Jupe grinned. "I'm Jupiter Jones. This is Pete Crenshaw and this is Bob Andrews. I suppose we'll start with the usual question, Mr. DeMento. Is there anyone in particular you suspect?"

"Anyone—or rather everyone." Madman Dan motioned toward the crowd that had gathered around his smoke-bombed stall. Then he spread his arms to take in the whole convention floor. "You've got some of the nuttiest people in California gathered in this room." He grinned. "I'm not saying you have to be crazy to collect comics, but it helps."

"And you're saying they're all suspects?"

DeMento shrugged. "All I can say is, something happens to people when they start to collect things. It doesn't matter *what* they collect. They just aren't quite normal about it."

"You mean they might even steal," Jupe said. "Could the thief sell those books?"

"It wouldn't be easy with something like *Fan Fun*." Madman Dan frowned. "A single book of that value makes dealers nervous. They'd want to know where it came from."

"And the thief couldn't tell them that," Pete said.

DeMento nodded. "Problem is, you're dealing with collectors. The thief may keep the book in his basement for the rest of his life."

As the Investigators chewed over that fact, the bystanders around DeMento's stall were shooed away by hotel staffers, and the regular traffic started again. A twelve-year-old kid walked by with a sheet of thin cardboard covered with panels of black-and-white artwork. "Look what I got," he called to a friend. "A full page of Steve Tresh art from *Crimson Phantom*. Only seventy bucks."

A tall, thin sandy-haired man came forward. His skin was very pale, as if he never went outdoors. "Hey, kid," he said. "I'll give you seventy-five dollars for that."

"No way," the kid replied.

"Okay." The pale man snatched the illustration board with one hand while shoving a fistful of bills at the kid with the other. "That's a hundred bucks," he said. "Enjoy it."

While the kid gaped, the man tore up the illustration and dropped the pieces in an ashtray. Then he pulled out a cigarette lighter and set the pieces on fire.

"Who do you think you are?" the kid yelled. "You have no right to do that!"

A short, fat guy with dark hair and a thick black beard stepped forward. "He has every right. That's Steve Tresh. He wrote and drew those panels."

The kid's jaw dropped. "*You're* Steve Tresh!" he gasped. "Can you sign my convention program?"

Smiling, the pale man scribbled on the kid's program.

"Too bad I couldn't have gotten it on that artwork," the kid said.

The smile disappeared from Steve Tresh's face. "I never autograph Crimson Phantom stuff." He turned away.

The fat guy shook his head at the kid. "You're batting two for two," he said. "Don't you know Tresh got cheated out of that series? Heroic Comics sells all his artwork, and he gets nothing for it. He'd rather burn his art than make it more valuable."

"Steve!" Dan DeMento called to the artist. "I've been wanting to meet you. I had a real collector's item here I wanted you to see." He grimaced. "But it got stolen."

"Hah!" The bearded fat guy walked over to the stall. "A thief complaining about getting robbed. That's rich."

DeMento glared at the man. "Get off my back, Carne."

"You take comics people love and make them pay through the nose for them," Carne accused. "It's people like you who ruin collecting—you and your outrageous prices."

Madman Dan started around the table of his stall, but Steve Tresh grabbed his arm. Jupe could see the convention stamp on the back of the artist's hand as his grip tightened. "Why don't you stay back there," Tresh advised. "Frank here has a point about the business side of comics—and everyone knows that us artists never see any money from all the work you guys sell."

"Gentlemen! Gentlemen!" Axel Griswold hurried over, wringing his slender hands. "I just got news of what happened, DeMento." He shook his head. "Wouldn't you know, this had to happen while I was off the floor. What did the thief get?"

"Nothing much. The best piece was an old fanzine, *Fan Fun* Number One, with some of Steve's work in it." Madman Dan pulled free from Tresh. "I'd hoped to show it to him."

"I know you have differences of opinion about selling comics," Griswold said to DeMento, Tresh, and Carne. "But I'm sure you don't like the idea of thieves in this convention. I hope I can depend on your help."

"Sure. We'll keep our eyes open," Frank Carne promised. "Come on, Steve. It's almost time to catch the beginning of *Rock Asteroid*." They headed off.

"I've already got some detectives at work on this thing," DeMento said. He introduced the Three Investigators to Griswold.

The red-haired convention boss looked at their card quickly. "Detectives, huh? Well, if there's anything I can do to help, let me know. Right now, though, I've got a new crisis to deal with. We were supposed to start a sixty-hour marathon screening of all four *Rock Asteroid* serials in the Gold Room—but the projectionist didn't show. Frank's going to have a wait."

He sighed. "I got the projector set up, but now I need a volunteer to run it. And the costume contest is about to start too." Griswold rushed off, looking frazzled.

"*Rock Asteroid?*" Bob asked in confusion.

"A science-fiction series from the late forties, I think," Jupe answered. Parking his box of leftover comics with DeMento, he ran after Griswold. Pete and Bob followed. "Can you take a few seconds to help us? Who were those two men just now?"

"The thin, pale guy was Steve Tresh, an artist and writer," Griswold said. "The fat one was Frank Carne. He's a letter hack—writes to the letters pages of all the comics as Frank the Crank." Griswold smiled. "It's a fit name. He has a very big sense of his own importance, telling people the way things ought to be. A troublemaker."

"He seems very friendly with Tresh," Jupe said.

"They've corresponded a lot," Griswold explained. "Until about a month ago, Tresh lived in Ohio. I think he came out here hoping to make it in L.A. But he hasn't done any comics since he arrived."

He sighed. "It made me feel a little sorry for him. I invited him to the convention as guest of honor and even gave him a room. Maybe that was a mistake."

Griswold glanced at his watch. "Sorry, guys, got to go."

The Investigators watched Griswold hurry off.

"What a case," Pete said.

"I think we might have a suspect," Bob suggested.

"Frank Carne? Or Steve Tresh?" Jupe asked.

"I was thinking of Tresh. The theft was outrageous—just like the way he handled that kid with his art," Bob said. "Maybe he didn't like the art in *Fan Fun* either."

"But he turned up right after the comic was stolen," Pete pointed out. "The smoke had barely cleared."

"Well, we know where he's staying," Jupe said. "Why don't we go up to his room and make sure there isn't a smoky comic lying around?"

Jupe got Tresh's room number from the reception desk. Three minutes later the Investigators were standing outside the door of room 318.

Jupe shook his head. "I don't think we can get past this lock," he said. "Not without special equipment."

He turned away, scowling. Then his face brightened

as he noticed that the door to room 320 was ajar. A maid's cart stood outside it.

Two quick knocks and a "Hello?" later, they were inside the empty hotel room.

"What do we do now?" Pete wanted to know. "Bore through the wall?"

"I don't think that will be necessary." Jupe headed to the sliding-glass door and stepped outside onto the balcony. The room overlooked the hotel's central courtyard and swimming pool. But Jupe's eyes went to the left—to the balcony of room 318, about four feet away. "It looks like a short enough jump. We just need someone athletic. A football hero, maybe."

"Oh, no," Pete began. "Not me."

Moments later he was climbing over the steel railing onto the very edge of room 320's balcony. "How do I let you guys talk me into these things?" he muttered. Both of his hands gripped the rail, which bit into the backs of his thighs. As usual, the other guys had stuck him in the jock role—fetch, carry, and now jump.

"Just think of it as a short broad jump," Bob suggested.

"Yeah," Pete grumbled. "Four feet across, but thirty feet down."

He balanced himself on his toes and let go of the railing. Resolutely keeping his eyes on the balcony across from him and off the ground three stories below, Pete jumped.

The other balcony came up. Pete's right foot

landed, but his left foot skidded off the edge. For a heart-stopping second he lurched over, but his hands grabbed the railing. White-knuckled, he pulled himself to safety. He swung over the rail, and when both feet were firmly set on the balcony, he glanced back at his friends. Jupe was pointing impatiently at the sliding-glass door to the room. "Glad to see you were so worried about me," Pete said sourly.

He crossed the balcony and peered through the door. The room looked empty. He tried the door. It slid open without a noise.

Pete stepped inside, scanning the room to make sure Tresh wasn't there. All he saw were piles of illustration board covered with pen-and-ink drawings—artwork Tresh obviously hoped to sell at the convention. Pete flipped through the material, but he didn't see the copy of *Fan Fun*.

He pulled open the door to the closet to see if the red robe was hanging inside. It wasn't. Then Pete turned to search through the dresser. As he pulled open the first drawer he saw movement behind him in the mirror.

Pete whirled—and froze. Leaping from the bathroom was a nightmare figure, a human body with a huge muscular bare chest, tight black jeans, and a fiendishly distorted green lizard's face—the Frog Mutant!

Too late, Pete realized that he was facing a plain, ordinary crook in a monster mask. Before he could even get his hands up, a fist caught him on the cheek.

He staggered back, knocking his head on the framework of the balcony door.

Half-blinded by pain, Pete tried an open-handed chop on his attacker, but he was hurting too much for more than a feeble counterattack. The Frog Mutant blocked it easily. Then he answered with a roundhouse right that sent Pete flying backward, dazed, right out the door.

Pete hit the balcony railing and went tumbling over, with nothing to stop his fall—except the ground below.

4

Astounding Stories

PETE TOPPLED HEADFIRST INTO THE COURTYARD BELOW. Desperately twisting in midair, he managed to take control of his wild tumble. He arched as widely as possible, aiming for the swimming pool. His Olympic-height dive would never have won a medal, but it gave him a safe splashdown.

Pete swam to the surface, gasping and sputtering, still shaken by his narrow escape. At the edge of the pool dozens of arms reached out to him. But Pete stayed where he was, treading water in shock.

Had he landed on another planet? Everyone in front of him looked like an extra from *Star Wars*. He saw robots, green people, characters with a couple of extra heads, and something that looked like a walking furry armchair.

Then he remembered—the costume contest! He'd dropped right into the middle of it. And judging from the dirty looks some of the contestants were giving him, he'd also managed to drench a lot of the people standing at poolside.

Still, some friendly types were on hand to help pull him out—including Jupe and Bob.

"What happened?" Bob asked as he and Jupe steered their dripping friend away from the crowd. "One second you were walking in. Then you came flying out."

"In between I walked into a fist—with plenty of muscle behind it," Pete reported.

"Tresh?" Bob asked. "Or the Crimson Phantom?"

Pete shook his head. "I don't think Tresh was the Phantom. There was no trace of the costume in his room. And the guy who hit me was built like a moose. He had muscles on top of muscles. But I didn't see his face. He was wearing a Frog Mutant mask."

"So we now have a hero stealing comics and a villain breaking into Tresh's room," Jupe said. "I wonder if they're connected."

"We've got company," Bob warned quietly. A man in a hotel blazer—obviously the manager from the insignia on the pocket—came marching toward them. He didn't look friendly. Also running up was Axel Griswold.

"Exactly what happened here?" the manager demanded.

"I—um—fell," Pete said.

"Fell? How? From where?" The manager loomed over Pete, who had dropped into one of the plastic poolside chairs.

"I—" Pete looked around desperately.

"I think you should sue," Jupe cut in. "Those

railings on the balconies are too short and shaky. My friend sneezes, steps back, and goes right over. You're lucky he's an athlete and was able to land safely."

The manager gave Jupe a cold stare. "Are you guests here?" he asked. "What room are you in?"

Axel Griswold stepped forward. "Room 316," he said. "They're with me."

Jupe let Griswold do the talking.

"Ah. I see." The manager turned to the convention chief. "This has not been a pleasant day so far, Mr. Griswold. First the robbery, now this . . . incident. I hope we won't have any more problems." He strode off.

"You and me both," Griswold said. He turned to Jupe. "This had something to do with your investigation, I hope?"

"It did," Jupe assured him. "Pete got jumped while checking something out. Thanks for helping. But if the manager looks for us in room 316 . . ."

"He'll find you. I was going to offer the room to you anyway. It's connected to my suite next door—314. I figured you'd need a place to crash if you were going to stay on the case." Griswold handed Jupe a room key. "Besides, your friend needs a place to dry off—unless that's his costume for Soggyman. Which reminds me." Griswold sighed. "I've got to tell the judges to get this costume show on the road."

He headed for the judges' stand, and the guys went up to room 316. The room contained two double beds, a dresser, and a locked door leading to room

314. Bob and Jupe left Pete wrapped up in towels with his clothes dripping into the bathtub, then headed downstairs again.

The convention hand-stamper was now a pimply-faced guy with a shock of unruly hair. The door guard was the girl with two-toned hair who'd stamped their hands before. She passed Jupe with little more than a glance. But she held on to Bob's hand, smiling up at him.

"Hi, my name's Lori," the girl said.

Bob flashed her his most charming smile. "Lori. That's my favorite name. Lori, did you see a guy in a Crimson Phantom costume leave after those smoke bombs went off?"

Lori gazed into Bob's eyes and shook her head.

Jupe interrupted to ask Lori if she'd seen anyone fitting Frank Carne's description. He wanted to check where Carne had been—and see what the guy could tell them.

Lori scowled at Jupe. "Do you know how many fat guys collect comics?" she snapped. "They range from plump to el grosso. And about nine hundred of them passed here."

"This guy is semifamous," Bob said. "He's a letter hack with a beard . . ."

"Oh, you mean Frank the Crank? Why didn't your friend say so? He came out of here just a couple of minutes ago, heading for the restaurant."

The guys were able to catch up with Carne in the restaurant line. He invited them to join him for lunch. "Let's get an outside table," he said. "Maybe we'll catch more of the show."

Jupe, thinking of another chance to see the blond girl, agreed eagerly.

Bob, thinking of Pete's swan dive, muttered, "I hope not."

They actually got a poolside table. Sitting under its umbrella, they watched the costume contest. As each contestant was announced, he or she would parade around the pool.

Carne ordered two cheeseburgers with the works. Bob contented himself with one. Jupe screwed up his face in pain as he read the menu. "Do you have . . . alfalfa sprouts?" he finally asked the waiter.

"Another diet, Jupe?" Bob tried to hide his smile. His friend had become as famous for his weird methods of trying to lose weight as he was for his detective brain.

"Alfalfa sprouts and a two-mile walk every day," Jupe admitted. "Supposed to melt the pounds off." He looked at the waiter, who shook his head negatively. "No alfalfa sprouts? I'll have a plain green salad—no dressing."

"I don't understand why you kids go around starving yourselves." Carne took a big bite out of his first burger, slurping up the fried onions that hung out over his lips. "Sure you don't want a bite?"

Jupe quickly changed the subject. "What we really need is information about the comics scene. Maybe you could give us some of the low-down."

"Low-down is a good way to describe this business," Carne said, a frown appearing under his heavy beard. "It's set up to rook collectors."

While he talked, an overweight guy in a metal box that looked like a giant toaster waddled around the pool.

Carne sighed. "I got into collecting because I love comics. When I see one with good art or writing, I write in to its letters page. So many people get involved in comics because they love them—then they get ground up by the business end. You saw Steve Tresh burn that art, didn't you?"

Jupe nodded, but his eyes were elsewhere. He'd just spotted the blond girl walking around the pool. Jupe had to pull himself together to listen to Carne.

"Steve's a classic case. Ten years ago, when he was eighteen, Steve invented a hero. Wrote the story, drew it, and got it published in a fanzine—a comic put out by fans. He called his character the Gray Phantom." Carne grinned. "He had to. Most fanzines appear in black and white. So you've got a choice of three colors—black, white, or gray. Anyway, the Gray Phantom was a real sensation, and Steve was discovered. Heroic Comics offered Steve a job, and his hero became—"

"The Crimson Phantom," Bob said. "I used to read that."

"It was a great book. Not just the art, which was fantastic—Steve can really draw. But the stories were wonderful. The Crimson Phantom was a different kind of hero. He didn't run around in long johns. He had those marvelous robes. And then there was the whole secret identity thing."

Bob nodded. "That's right. It really was a secret. *Nobody* knew who the Crimson Phantom was. There were three or four possible characters who might be his secret identity. I remember going crazy looking for clues."

"That book was one of the best comics ever made," Carne said flatly. "Till they ruined it."

"Ruined it?" Jupe asked. "How?"

"Tresh worked with an editor named Leo Rottweiler. He trusted Leo, and Leo got him to sign away his rights to the character. Then Rottweiler totally took over the book, making sure it was 'popular.' " Carne thumped the table. "He started the contest to vote for the secret identity."

Bob looked a little embarrassed. "I remember voting," he said.

"Sure, it was designed to suck in more kid readers. Then he started up two new Crimson Phantom books—*Secrets of the Crimson Phantom* and *The Battling Crimson Phantom*. That meant bringing in new writers and artists. They weren't bad . . . just *ordinary*."

Carne scowled. "Leo killed everything that was special about the character. *The Crimson Phantom* is still around today, selling well. But it's just another comic. Of course, it made Leo Rottweiler the resident genius at Heroic Comics."

"What about Steve Tresh?" Jupe asked as another costumed guy passed their table. He looked like a walking version of Jupe's salad.

"When Tresh saw what they did to his character, he tried to stop it. He couldn't, so he quit. Since then he's had nothing to do with Heroic Comics—or the Crimson Phantom. You saw how he won't even autograph any of his old artwork. Heroic owned it and sold it. Steve would rather burn that stuff than see it sold."

"So you're saying the comic companies cheat comic lovers," Jupe said.

"Kid, *everybody* cheats comic lovers. And we collectors help them." Carne looked around and spotted a dark-haired young man eating at a nearby table. "Hey, Hunter, you have a copy of *Overstreet?*"

The guy put down his burger, dug in his knapsack, and came up with a battered copy of the thick book. "Catch," he yelled, tossing it over.

Frank the Crank caught the book and thumbed through it. "Here it is—*Cerebus.* This is a black-and-white comic, first issue published back in 1977. A mint copy goes for five hundred dollars. But see this under here? A counterfeit copy was made. This mark tells how to recognize it—and says the counterfeits are worth twenty to thirty bucks!"

He shook his head as he handed back the book. "Fans even reward the people who cheat them. They turn counterfeits into collector's items."

Carne frowned again. "And, of course, there are

friendly neighborhood dealers who sell the counterfeits as the real thing."

Jupe looked up. "Like who?"

"I've heard people complain about deals with Dan DeMento," Carne said. "If you're going to deal with Madman Dan, check your watch after you shake his hand."

Just then, the PA system at the pool whined, and the judges announced the winners of the costume contest. First prize went to a guy completely wrapped in fake fur as Slorz the Planet Eater.

At the next table Hunter made a disgusted sound. "What I want to know is why that blond chick didn't win."

Jupe was wondering the same thing as he stared at the girl, but he didn't speak.

Carne got up. "Uh-oh, gotta go. The Muckmen are about to disintegrate Rock's ship."

The Investigators stared as Carne hurried off to pay his bill. Hunter burst out laughing at the looks on their faces. "It's *Rock Asteroid*," he explained. "Frank's seen the movies so often, he only shows up for the good parts."

Rising from the table, Bob muttered, "What a bunch of characters. Is everyone here weird?"

They headed out. From the corner of his eye Jupe caught a flash of gold.

He turned to see the blond girl sitting down at a table near the restaurant entrance. She was with an older woman—probably her mother. As Jupe got nearer he recognized the third person at her table. It was the bald older man who'd tried to buy the copy of *Fan Fun* from Dan DeMento.

Working his way toward the door, Jupe was close enough to overhear the conversation at the table.

The older woman was patting the girl's shoulder as she talked to the bald man. "I think you should go for some photo covers on *Stellara Stargirl*—and here's the perfect model for you, Mr. Rottweiler."

So that's Leo Rottweiler, Jupe thought. I wonder why he's so interested in Steve Tresh's early work.

He turned to join Bob, who was paying the cashier for their lunch. Then a loud, angry voice made him turn again.

Steve Tresh stood red-faced in the restaurant entrance, shouting.

"What's going on around here, Griswold? I just went up to my room—and somebody trashed the place!"

5

Weird People

"STEVE, DO WE HAVE TO TALK ABOUT THIS RIGHT HERE?" Axel Griswold, the convention boss, stood framed in the restaurant doorway looking very embarrassed. A circle of convention-goers gathered, looking extremely interested as Tresh shoved at him.

Jupe and Bob joined the crowd as Steve Tresh started yelling, "Somebody got into my room, tore up my clothes—and slashed all my artwork."

A gasp rose from the conventioneers.

"Why would anyone do a thing like that?" Griswold asked.

"That's what I want to know. Where was your security? What kind of convention is this?"

Griswold tried to calm the artist down. "I can understand how upset you are. If you want to leave . . ."

"Leave?" Tresh's voice rose. "*I* don't want to leave. What I want is that guy—do you know how much of my artwork he ruined? I came here to earn money. And that's what I'm going to do—if I have to make doodles at ten bucks a shot."

He strode away, then turned back. "If you want to find me, I'll be out on the convention floor—*drawing*."

The crowd broke up, everyone buzzing. Jupe and Bob joined Griswold, who was shaking his head. "See that?" he said. "Even comic-book artists have artistic temperaments."

He shrugged. "Or rent to pay. The main reason Steve agreed to come was the chance of selling his artwork. He must really be hard up if he's willing to stay on after it's been destroyed."

Jupe nodded. Lack of money also made a good motive for theft. "I wanted to ask you about some other people," he said. "Who's that girl in the gold costume?"

Griswold smiled. "Oh, you mean Rainey Fields. She's a cute kid. This is her first major convention. You've got to admit, she makes a perfect Stellara Stargirl." He leaned forward and added confidentially, "Her mother's really pushing for little Rainey to become a star."

"Who's the man at the table?" Jupe asked him.

"That's Leo Rottweiler. He's a senior editor at Heroic Comics. They publish *Stellara Stargirl*. You've got to hand it to Ma Fields. She knows who to go after and how to get them. Don't be surprised if in a couple of months you see Rainey's face smiling at you from some comic rack."

He shook his head. "That woman is a public relations genius. I wish she would work for me."

Griswold reached into his pocket. "If you want to meet them, come to the banquet tonight. I've got some extra tickets. One for you . . ." He handed one to Bob. "One for you . . ." He handed one to Jupe. "And one," he said with a grin, "for your damp friend upstairs.

"It'll be quite a bash," Griswold added. "I expect it to run pretty late. But you guys don't have to worry. You've got a room for the night."

He glanced at his watch. "Got to run. I'm supposed to be introducing the Fan Guest of Honor to the press." He dashed off.

"What's a Fan Guest of Honor?" Bob asked.

Jupe just shook his head. "I don't know why Griswold thinks he needs a PR person. He seems to do a great job all by himself."

Bob grinned. "So what's our next move?"

"Let's go upstairs and get Pete. Then we'll head back home. Pete needs dry clothes, and I suspect we all need something a little better than jeans and T-shirts for this banquet."

Pete's clothes were still slightly soggy, but he pulled them on, uncomplaining, and got his car. As they drove to Rocky Beach Jupe asked, "Who gets your votes for top suspect?"

"Still Steve Tresh," Bob said.

"Why?"

Bob glanced back at Jupe from the front seat. "I can't get the picture of him burning his own artwork out of my head. Looks like he's got something to prove. And we know that his work was in that *Fan Fun* book that got stolen."

"That's a point," Jupe agreed.

"Then there's the fact that he seems to be short of money. He freaked out when his pictures were ruined. But if he needs money, why did he shell out the hundred bucks to pay for the art he burned? He's definitely acting weird."

"Okay, let's say Tresh is our thief," Jupe said. "How does wrecking his room fit in?"

"I'm not sure," Bob said. "But it establishes Tresh as a victim and an unlikely suspect. And now everybody knows there are no stolen comics in the room. Even if Tresh were suspected, the evidence would be gone. I wonder if the Crimson Phantom and the frog guy who jumped Pete were both Tresh?"

"No way," said Pete from behind the wheel. "Tresh is built like a basketball forward. The masked guy in his room had a build like a linebacker."

"Could it have been Frank Carne?" Jupe asked.

Pete frowned. "Nah. I saw this guy's chest. He had muscles. The only muscles Carne has are in his mouth."

"There are other people involved in this Crimson Phantom thing as well—DeMento and Rottweiler." Jupe leaned back in his seat. "Have you noticed how everyone contradicts everybody else? Carne thinks Tresh is a genius. DeMento kind of thinks he's a nut, and Griswold feels sorry for him. DeMento thinks of himself as a businessman; Carne and Tresh think he's a crook."

Bob laughed. "Carne thinks he's a reformer, trying to save comics. Griswold and DeMento think he's a troublemaker." He thought for a second. "How about Rottweiler? I don't think anybody likes him. Tresh must hate him for stealing his hero. Carne thinks he ruined the *Crimson Phantom*. And DeMento certainly gave him a hard time when he tried to buy that fanzine."

"Does it mean something that the book he tried to buy is the one that got stolen?" Pete asked.

"It would make him suspect number two, if I could believe he'd attack you," Jupe told Pete. "But Rottweiler looks like a stork with a potbelly. Not exactly the muscleman you described."

Jupe scowled up at the ceiling of the car. He wanted to add Rainey Fields to the list of suspects. Then he'd have a great excuse to talk to her. But what was she guilty of? Walking past Madman Dan's stall while Jupe was trying to bargain with him?

Of course, it's the oldest trick in the book—send a pretty girl past the scene of a crime to distract all the witnesses, Jupe told himself.

Somehow that didn't make him feel better. In fact, he'd feel pretty miserable if Rainey were involved in the crime.

"This case is weird," Bob finally said.

Jupe nodded. "I guess what Dan DeMento told us about collectors being a little crazy is true," he said.

"And I don't think it helps that what they collect is something as childish as comic books."

"Right," Bob agreed dryly. "If they were smart, they'd collect electronic stuff. Computers are much more mature."

With a spreading grin Bob went on. "Or maybe they ought to collect cars."

Jupe gave his friend a look. "Maybe they should just collect girls, like a certain person I know."

That ended discussion of the case.

When they pulled into Rocky Beach, Pete dropped Jupe off at his house across the street from the junkyard. Jupe caught both his aunt and uncle in and told them he'd be staying overnight at the hotel. Then he spent some time getting a change of clothes together—as well as a jacket and slacks for the banquet.

Within half an hour the other Investigators returned with their overnight bags. Jupe got into Pete's Impala and they headed for the Coast Highway. As they drove back to L.A., Jupe asked Pete to detour through Santa Monica.

"You probably noticed that the sign on Madman Dan's stall said his shop was in Santa Monica," Jupe said. "I looked in the phone book to get the address and saw it wasn't far off our route. I thought we might check the place out—see what kind of operation he's running."

Madman Dan's Comix Emporium was on Pico Boulevard, a simple storefront on the edge of the commercial district. It stood between an unprosperous-looking shop that sold handmade wicker furniture and one that sold vacuum cleaners.

Dan DeMento's store was a blaze of color. The windows were plastered with posters of gaudily-costumed heroes and villains squaring off against each other. Over the door was a poster of Stellara Stargirl soaring high. She really did look like Rainey Fields. Or was it the other way around?

"Well, well," said Pete, pulling up alongside a green van. "Look who's here."

Leaning against the van as two kids staggered out of the store under boxes of comics was Dan DeMento.

"Mr. DeMento!" Jupe called as he got out of the car.

"Oh. You guys." Madman Dan ran a hand through his wild hair, then started riffling through the plastic-wrapped comics he was holding.

"Getting more stock for the convention, I see," Jupe said. "And I guess the comics in your hands will fill in the hole the thief made."

"You deduced right," DeMento said, squaring up the little pile. "I hear one of you guys found a clue about gravity, too. When you fall off a balcony, you wind up in a swimming pool." He shook his head. "Are you guys sure you're detectives?"

Jupe looked down. His glance scanned the cover of the top comic in DeMento's hand. Another copy of *Fan Fun* Number One. What caught Jupe's eye, however, was the price sticker on the bag. Two hundred and fifty dollars.

"I see you're replacing the book that was stolen," he said. "But the price is a lot lower than what you quoted to Leo Rottweiler."

"That was a special book," DeMento began. Then he stopped short. "Why are you questioning me? You should be trying to find that thief."

"We've been investigating," Jupe said. "Talking to people."

"Talking to the *wrong* people, if you ask me," DeMento said. "My friends saw you in the restaurant with Frank the Crank. Don't pay too much attention to that guy. Guys like Frank Carne and Steve Tresh never grow up. I started like them, collecting. But when I made collecting my business, I learned to act like a businessman instead of a kid."

He frowned. "Those guys hold grudges that aren't even sensible. It's the comic dealers and comic shops that keep cult guys like Tresh in business. Does he see that? No. He and Carne just love to see guys like me suffer."

Jupe nodded. The question was, would they go as far as theft to *make* DeMento suffer?

6

Arts—and Craftiness

THE INVESTIGATORS LEFT DEMENTO AT HIS STORE AND drove to the Century Grand. Pete sighed from behind the wheel. "I guess I didn't help us very much when I took that fall," he said. "Looks like DeMento thinks of us as the Three Stooges instead of the Three Investigators."

"We'll just have to make him forget that." Jupe sat up in his seat. "And the way to do it is some heavy-duty legwork. We've got to find out who was where when those comics were stolen."

"We know where DeMento was," Bob said. "He was standing in front of us."

And we know where Rainey Fields was—heading away from us as the Crimson Phantom approached. Maybe I should ask her . . . Jupe pushed that thought to the back of his mind as he went over the other possible suspects. "I'd like to know where Leo Rottweiler was. And Frank the Crank. Most especially, where was Steve Tresh when the crime went down? *That* might tell us something."

They parked in the underground garage, took the elevator to their room, and dropped off their stuff. Then they headed for the main conference room. Jupe thought the crowd outside the convention doors had thinned a little. But the madhouse inside seemed even more jam-packed than before. The husky security guard with the chipped tooth was back in position. He blocked their way and checked the stamp marks on their hands.

Jupe led his pals through the crowd toward the far end of the room. The mob scene grew denser as they came to a row of tables. Behind the tables sat artists, sketching and signing autographs. Some of the tables had posters set up on them, as well as books, comics, magazines, and piles and piles of illustration board with comic panels.

The artists seemed to be doing a landslide business. Hundreds of people were lined up in front of them, from kids clutching old comics to middle-aged men with fat wallets coming to buy artwork. Most of the fans were shiny-eyed at the chance to meet their artist-heroes. But some were out of hand, pawing through the artwork for things to buy and demanding autographs on everything from T-shirts to cardboard coffee cups.

In between autograph requests the conversations were equally outrageous. "*Slime Man* just hasn't been the same without you, Jack," a fevered fan told one artist. "Nobody draws slime like you do."

Another young fan came up to an artist and yelled,

"You ruined *Robot Avenger*. Stebbins knew how to draw robots. You made the robot's head look like a Volvo. They ought to can you from that book. Oh, and by the way, can you sign these pages for me?"

The artist stared at the kid. "If you don't like my work, why are you collecting it?"

"I can get twice what I paid for this with your autograph on it," the kid said without batting an eye.

Shaking his head, the artist signed.

Jupe couldn't believe it. "I guess it's one way to ditch a fan," he said. "Let's find Steve Tresh."

Tresh was engulfed by the longest line of all. The pasty-faced artist sat at a bare table, quickly dashing off sketches of various heroes and villains. Some of his fans had come by to sympathize at the way his artwork had been destroyed. They were happy to buy new sketches.

Some of the younger kids were demanding that Tresh draw Crimson Phantom sketches or autograph Crimson Phantom comic books for them. "C'mon!" one teenager yelled, waving a comic in the artist's face. "What else are ya famous for? Sign this!"

Tresh grabbed the kid's wrist. "I've worked on twenty other characters besides the Crimson Phantom—other people's and my own. If you want a signature for that comic, get Leo Rottweiler's. It's his book now."

"Everybody autographs things," the loudmouth insisted. "You gotta."

"No, I don't." Tresh shook his head. "And if you

keep shoving that book in my face, I might 'accidentally' spill a bottle of ink all over it."

The teenager still waved the book.

"It might even accidentally get torn in two."

The pushy fan snatched the book back and disappeared into the crowd.

"Let me take a crack at Tresh," Bob whispered to the other Investigators. He wormed his way through the crush. Lots of heads turned to give him dirty looks, but he kept moving. How would he get Tresh's attention? Finally he decided on the direct approach.

"Mr. Tresh!"

Steve Tresh glanced up. "What now?" He looked at Bob's empty hands. "At least you don't have anything idiotic for me to sign, so I guess you want a sketch. Who can I do for you? I'd say you were a Killer Brain fan. Am I right?" His pen was already dashing over the paper.

"Speaking of killers, I saw you in action right after Dan DeMento's stall got ripped off. That was an incredible move, snatching the art from that kid."

Tresh's pen skidded to a stop.

"Too bad you weren't around when the comics were snatched," Bob went on. "You might have caught the guy who grabbed them. Where were you right then? Did you see him?"

Tresh stared at Bob in silence. The artist's fans started getting annoyed. "Hey, chump!" one called out. "You want to talk to the man, wait your turn like everybody else."

"C'mon, Steve," another yelled. "We've got business to do. Get rid of this guy."

"Where was I?" Tresh finally said to Bob. "In the middle of this zoo, right here." His voice turned sour as his pen started scribbling again. "At least then I had artwork to sell. Get lost, will you? I'm busy right now."

He held up his sketch. "Anybody want to buy a Killer Brain?"

Bob stared, taken aback by the quick way he'd been dismissed. But then, he realized, Tresh had lots of practice with this unruly crew. Dozens of voices were shouting in his ears, bidding for the picture. Bob just managed to lean over and flip a business card to Tresh. "Maybe we can talk again," he said. Then he started to squash his way out of the mob.

Jupe and Pete were waiting on the fringes of the crowd right where Bob had left them.

"What did he say?" Pete asked.

"Tresh said he was right there," Bob said, glancing back at the crowd. "If the same mob was around, he'd have a lot of witnesses." Bob tried to pull his polo shirt straight, but for once his tidy image was completely shot.

"Nice claim." Jupe's eyes narrowed. "But then how did he turn up at DeMento's stall so soon after the robbery?"

"He and Frank Carne showed up at the same time," Bob said. "Maybe they were together."

Jupe nodded. "Good point. Now, where do we find Carne?"

A familiar face suddenly appeared in the crowd—
Hunter, the dealer who had lent Carne his copy of
Overstreet. "Hey, guys," he said. "What's happen-
ing?"

But when he heard their question, he shook his
head. "I haven't seen Frank the Crank for an hour."
He suddenly grinned. "You could try staking out the
Gold Room. Head out the front, hang a left, another
left, and go all the way down the hallway. Sooner or
later Frank will turn up for one of the good parts of
Rock Asteroid."

"Thanks," Jupe said. "and how about Leo Rottweiler? Have you seen him?"

"Sure," Hunter said, pointing. "He's over there
with a bunch of Heroic people—some kind of PR
stunt for their new Heroic Classics series."

Jupe followed Hunter's arm to catch the flash of
cameras— and the glint of a gold costume. He quickly
led the way to a cleared area where a group of Heroic
Comics artists were posing beside life-size cardboard
cutouts of their characters.

But the cameras and TV lights were all clustered
around the cutout of Stellara Stargirl. The reason
didn't take much detection. Standing next to it was
Rainey Fields, still in costume, giving a dazzling smile
to the news people.

Her mother stood on the sidelines talking sweetly to
all the reporters nearby. And behind her, looking torn
between delight over the news coverage and annoyance at being upstaged, was Leo Rottweiler.

Jupe stepped up to the editor. "Mr. Rottweiler, could I ask you a question?"

"Why not, kid?" Rottweiler ran a hand over his bald head. "Nobody else seems to be."

"I noticed you were at Dan DeMento's stall shortly before the theft," Jupe said. "Do you think the comic you were looking at was worth stealing?"

Rottweiler stared at him. "What kind of question is that? And where do you get off asking it?"

"My friends and I are investigating the case for Mr. DeMento." Jupe handed Rottweiler a business card. "I wanted your expert opinion . . ."

"You want more than that." Rottweiler flicked a finger against the card and glared at Jupe. "I wasn't even on the convention floor, much less near that stall when it was robbed. Some idiot fan trapped me in an argument outside the Gold Room."

"A fan?" Jupe asked.

"Frank Carne." Rottweiler frowned, as if even the memory annoyed him. "He came out of the Gold Room, where they were showing that stupid movie. I guess there'd been some sort of foul-up with the projector. Axel Griswold was in there trying to fix it. Carne came out to bother me with his nonsense."

"And then?"

"Somebody came by and told us about the commotion at DeMento's stall. Carne went back to take a look at it. I figured Griswold should know about it, so I got him. Frankly, I was happy to get away from Carne. He has a very big opinion of himself." Rottweiler smiled nastily. "Almost as big as his waistline."

The editor turned away. "Now, if you'll excuse me, I have business—answering *legitimate* questions."

Jupe stared at the man as he walked off. It seemed to him he was seeing more backs in this case than anything else.

A hand landed on Jupe's shoulder and he turned to find Axel Griswold standing beside him.

"I saw you talking with Leo Rottweiler," the convention boss said. "Is he involved in your case?"

"Maybe," Jupe said. "He was at DeMento's stall right before the robbery. But he has an alibi for the actual robbery itself—which we'll have to check out."

"Who else have you been checking?"

"We want to find Frank Carne—and we've already spoken to Steve Tresh," Jupe said.

Griswold's eyes glowed with interest. "Does Steve have an alibi too?"

"He said he was over in the artists' section selling stuff. I suppose about nine hundred autograph seekers will back him up."

"I don't think so." Griswold was frowning. "Right before I met you guys at the entrance, I passed by the artists' area. I know for sure there was no crowd at Steve's table—because Steve Tresh wasn't there."

7

Dinner and a Show

"LET'S NAIL DOWN THOSE ALIBIS TONIGHT," JUPE SAID TO his friends as they stepped into the banquet room. "And I'd like to talk to some people who were around DeMento's stall at the time of the robbery." He nervously straightened his tie.

Pete's eyebrows went up. "*Some* people?" he said with a grin. "Like maybe that blonde who made your eyes pop out? I never saw such a struggle. Jupiter Jones making a money deal and being distracted by true love."

"Knock it off." Jupe's voice got gruff, and he could feel his cheeks turning red. But he hoped that Rainey Fields would be around.

She was, in another Stellara Stargirl outfit. This one was more formal, with a high-necked cape. Rainey's blond hair was done up in a fantastic headdress, and she'd added a skirt made from strips of gold silk to the basic outfit. Whenever she moved, it showed off her fantastic long legs. If anything, she turned even more heads in this costume than she had all day.

Jupe waited until Rainey's mother was deep in conversation with some comic-book biggie before he came over to talk.

"Hey, you're one of the guys tracking down the stolen comic books," Rainey said after Jupe introduced himself. Her big hazel eyes sparkled with interest. "Everyone on the convention floor has been talking about you—especially since your friend fell in the swimming pool."

"Ah—yes," Jupe replied. Great, he thought to himself. You're supposed to be questioning her and all you can come up with is "Ah—yes." Pull yourself together!

"At the approximate time of the robbery you were in the vicinity of the robbery site," Jupe found himself saying. This is worse, he thought. I sound just the way I did back when I was ten, trying to impress the grownups.

Rainey looked at him oddly.

"Dan DeMento's stall," Jupe went on, his collar suddenly feeling two sizes too small. "I personally observed—ah, I saw you there."

Rainey grinned. "I guess a lot of people were observing me. This getup is pretty hard to miss." She pulled the cape around herself. "I don't know where I got the nerve to enter the contest."

"You look admirable—um, fine," Jupe said.

"Do you always talk that way?" Rainey gave him a sideways look. "With instant translations?"

Only when I'm tripping over my tongue, Jupe

thought. But he managed to say, "It's the first time I ever interviewed a superbeing."

Rainey's grin turned to a full-out smile. "I didn't see the perpetrator—isn't that what they always call him?"

"But maybe you saw something—anything out of the ordinary."

Rainey shrugged. "I didn't really notice a thing. To tell the truth, I was fighting a bad case of stage fright. You see, this is my first big convention."

Tiny lines appeared on her forehead as she thought. "Wait. I remember Madman Dan's stall, because of that crazy name. There was a guy with frizzy black hair behind the table"—she glanced at Jupe—"and *you* were talking to him!" She concentrated some more. "There was a tall guy standing beside you—and a real cute blond guy."

Jupe sighed. Trust any girl to remember Bob.

"Did you notice anything else?"

Rainey shook her head. "Not really. I was on my way to that costume contest, and that's all I was thinking about. Oh. That guy in the Crimson Phantom costume breezed past me. He was going pretty fast—his robes billowed out. At least it wasn't Slime Man. Could you imagine him brushing past you?" She wrinkled her nose.

"Did you notice anything in particular about him?" Jupe asked.

"What was there to notice? He was a guy dressed as the Crimson Phantom—in a big hurry."

"Think for a minute," Jupe said. "Picture him in your mind. Tell me what he's doing."

Rainey closed her eyes. "He's reaching inside his costume—getting something out."

"He was probably pulling out the smoke bombs he dropped in front of the stand." Jupe looked at her closely. "Did you see what he was wearing under his costume?"

Frowning, Rainey shook her head. "Sorry. I really wasn't paying attention. I was too busy worrying about that dumb contest."

"When the bombs went off, there was a lot of yelling and screaming. Did you notice that?"

"Sure," said Rainey. "I looked back for a second. But I had to get to the contest, so I kept going. I was afraid I'd be late. Oh, and I saw the guy in the Crimson Phantom costume running."

Jupe leaned forward. "He brushed past you again?"

"No. I just caught a glimpse of red, heading away from me, like toward the exit."

"Where were you going?"

"You know where all the artists are sitting?" Rainey said. "At the far end of the room from the entrance? That's where they got us together for the contest."

"You're sure he was heading for the doors?"

Rainey shrugged. "There's no way I can be sure. I saw smoke, and a flash of red over somebody's shoulder—as if the robe was flapping. After that, I didn't see the guy again."

"Nobody at the entrance saw him," Jupe said.

"You'd think a man in a red robe would be hard to miss." He looked at Rainey, trying to think of something else to say. But nothing came into his head. "I guess those are all my questions."

"Can I take a turn now?" Rainey said with a grin.

"Oh—sure," Jupe said. She wants to talk, he thought to himself. This is a good sign.

"Your cute friend—does he like blondes?"

For a long second Jupe stared at Rainey. Then he heard a voice saying, "Oh, Rainey, dear."

"I think I hear your mother calling," Jupe said quickly. He handed Rainey one of the Investigators' business cards. "Maybe we'll talk again. Keep this— um—if your costume has pockets."

Rainey laughed. "I'll find someplace to tuck it away."

They let themselves be separated by the mingling crowd. A few minutes later Bob grabbed Jupe's arm. "I found Frank Carne."

Jupe grinned. He knew Bob would handle that job. "What does he say?"

"The same thing as Rottweiler. They were outside the Gold Room arguing."

"Over what?" Jupe wanted to know.

"Are you ready for this? Over the artwork in the latest *Crimson Phantom* books. Rottweiler brought in a new artist. Carne says this new guy stinks—he can't do shadows."

"Shadows?"

"When Tresh created the Crimson Phantom, he

used all sorts of spooky highlighting—especially the black shadows on the character's skull mask," Bob explained. "The new artist took them all out. Carne says he turned the Crimson Phantom from a menace into a wimpy coloring book character."

"Interesting," Jupe said. "Remember the mask on the thief? It had black shadows painted on. I guess Carne would approve."

"Approve?" Bob asked.

"For the moment, let's just say it's the kind of mask a purist would wear," Jupe suggested. "And here's another thing to remember. Billowing robes are a great disguise. You can't tell the shape of the guy under them." He patted his own ample stomach. "Now let's find Pete and get some seats."

"Seats are taken care of," Bob said. "Carne invited us to eat at his table."

"Okay, so where's Pete?" Jupe started scanning the crowd, when a bustle of movement caught his attention. Leo Rottweiler had just put a hand on Steve Tresh's chest. "You've got a smart mouth, Tresh. I've heard some of the remarks you've made about me."

"You don't like me calling you a crook?" the hot-tempered artist shot back. "Wait till you hear my speech!"

"That does it!" Rottweiler shoved Tresh backward and went to throw a punch. Tresh staggered into the crowd but came back, fists ready. The two men were actually swinging at each other when someone pushed between them.

It was the beefy security guy from the convention door, with a jacket over his black T-shirt. He grabbed Tresh and swung him away. Rottweiler landed a glancing blow to Tresh's cheek before Axel Griswold appeared and grabbed the editor's arm.

"Brave, Rottweiler, real brave," Tresh sneered. The convention staffers led the two men up on the dais, seating them at opposite ends. Taking that as a hint, the crowd members began finding their own seats.

Bob and Jupe found Pete and headed for Carne's table. Jupe looked back at the glowering artist. "What did you find out about Tresh, Pete?"

"Nobody saw him around the artists' tables at the time of the robbery," Pete reported.

"It was very confused around there, from what I hear," Jupe said. "That's where the people were assembling for the costume contest."

Pete shrugged. "I talked to a bunch of artists. They say he wasn't there."

"I'd say we have some more questions for Mr. Tresh," Bob said.

"Let's eat first," said Jupe. Then he looked forlornly at the wilted salad on the table. "Anyone want to trade their salad for the rest of my meal?"

Frank Carne, already at the table, was only too happy to oblige. Actually, Jupe made out well on the deal. The salad wasn't bad compared with dinner—rubber chicken with burned potatoes.

"Guess we can't complain," Bob whispered to Pete. "We got in for free."

They couldn't follow their after-dinner plan of questioning Tresh, either. As it turned out, he was the after-dinner speaker.

"I'd like to thank Axel Griswold for asking me to give you a few words," Tresh said with a smile. "It's the first time since I moved to California that anyone has paid for my words."

The audience gave him a mild laugh.

"I know some people think I've given up comics entirely since I came out here." Tresh shook his head. "They don't have to worry. I've been working on a new comics hero, and you'll be seeing him very soon."

Happy applause greeted this announcement.

"Who are you doing it for?" someone called out.

Tresh turned in the direction of the voice. "I'm not doing it 'for' anybody but myself. This time I'm publishing independently. Less corporate hassles that way. And"—his eyes flashed to Leo Rottweiler on the far end of the dais—"less chance of theft."

The editor's bald head was a dull shade of red as he glared at Tresh.

Steve Tresh went on to discuss the problems of self-publishing. When he finished, he was mobbed by an enormous crowd of eager fans.

At the Investigators' table, Frank Carne nodded approvingly. "I'd heard rumors that Steve was working on something," he said. "Glad to see it's for real." He combed his fingers through his beard thoughtfully. "I wonder where he's getting the money, though."

"I thought that's why he was here," Jupe said. "To make money."

"He'd need more than he'd make at a convention to finance a book of his own," Carne objected. "Independent publishing takes big bucks."

"Another question for Steve Tresh," Bob murmured.

Jupe nodded. Tresh had no alibi for the time of the crime. And now it seemed as if he had a motive—money.

Glancing over at Pete, Jupe caught his friend stifling a yawn. "I know how you feel," Jupe said. "What do you say we hold off on talking to Tresh and head up to room 316? I could use some sleep."

"Us, too," Bob and Pete agreed.

"Well, good night, guys," Frank the Crank said. "I'll be leaving pretty soon myself. It's coming up to where Rock zaps the Muckmen army with the blutellium bomb."

Shaking their heads, the Investigators left.

On their way out they passed the table where Rainey Fields sat. As usual, her mother was deep in conversation with somebody. Rainey looked over and smiled.

Was that smile for me? Jupe wondered. Or for Bob?

The thought continued to bother him even after he'd gotten into bed. From the regular breathing around him, he could tell his two friends were already asleep. But he lay in the darkened hotel room with Rainey's smiling face still appearing before his eyes.

She was friendly enough. Maybe, just maybe—He shook his head. Maybe I'm getting out of my league here. . . .

His thoughts were interrupted by a tiny rattle at the door to the room. Jupe sat up in bed. Somebody was trying to break in!

8

Attack of the Killer Cyclops

THE DOOR OPENED.

Jupe caught a glimpse of the intruder, a fuzzy figure silhouetted in the doorway. The door automatically swung shut behind him. The intruder was in the room.

Jupe's hand shot to the lamp on the bedside table. But in the dark and unfamiliar room, he misjudged the distance. The lamp fell over with a crash.

"Hey! What—" Both Bob and Pete were surprised to be awakened from a sound sleep. But when they realized there was an intruder, they jumped at him.

It was a confused battle in the darkness. Jupe took a swing, but found himself pulling his punch. What if I hit one of the guys by mistake? he thought.

The intruder had no such problem—anyone he hit was an enemy, so he hit hard.

As Jupe groped his way forward the unseen enemy lashed out, kicking Jupe in the stomach. Jupe gasped in pain and sat down hard. But he used his judo training to turn the drop into a controlled fall. Jupe rolled to his left, slapping the floor, and heaved himself upright. He headed for the wall. If he could just find the light switch . . .

He heard a grunt, then a sharp cry from Bob. "He's getting away!" More sounds of confused movement cut the darkness—and then Jupe's fingers found the switch!

The ceiling fixture came on, dazzling the Investigators—just as the intruder threw open the door and made a run for it.

"Come on!" The three tumbled through the door and headed down the hallway. Their quarry had already made it to the first bend. They rounded the turn, then stumbled to a surprised halt.

A long hallway stretched before them—longer than the intruder could have run. Yet nobody was there.

"Must have ducked into one of the rooms," Bob gasped. He had a hand to his side—he'd been kicked, too.

"Yeah. Or—" Pete ran to a small alcove in the hall, decorated with an EXIT sign. He threw the door open and heard the pounding sounds of fast movement. "He's taking the fire stairs! Let's go!"

Jupe could feel the metal stairs shaking as they thundered down. The guy ahead couldn't help but know they were still on his trail. Jupe just wanted to catch up with this guy. For their stolen comics, and for that foot in the gut. He could feel his hands turning into fists as he pushed himself to keep up with his friends.

The stairs ended at the entrance to the hotel's underground garage.

Together the guys rammed into the panic bar on the door, throwing it open to reveal one of the darker corners of the complex. Heavy pillars blocked out most of the nearby light, and the ceiling fixture over the door had a broken bulb.

Pete dashed forward, eager to have it out with the intruder. He turned left on the concrete floor, yelling, "This way!"

Legs pumping, he outdistanced his friends, rapidly gaining on the dark figure. "He's mine!" he shouted to the others. "For punch . . . on . . . balcony!"

Pete took a final giant step, then hurled himself forward in a tackle. It should have brought down the intruder.

Instead, the shadowy figure turned and caught Pete in midair with a backhand slam. Pete bounced into one of the concrete pillars, then disappeared behind it.

"Pete!" Bob skidded to a halt and knelt beside his friend. "Are you all right?"

"Knocked the breath out of me," Pete gasped, pushing himself up. "Come on!"

Bringing up the rear, Jupe had seen Bob stop for Pete. Now he was the advance guard as he rounded the pillar. He ran about five more steps, when he was blinded by the high beams of a car's headlights.

Make that *headlight*. The car in front of him was a Cyclops—only one light worked. And judging from the size of it, it was probably a van.

But if the van's lights didn't both work, its engine was fine. It roared to life as the driver gunned the gas, sending the vehicle leaping straight at Jupe!

He barely had time to shout a warning as he flung himself aside. Bob and Pete, just rounding the pillar, spilled to the ground as the van screeched past them.

Jupe leaped to his feet and raced after the van. But it was already squealing up the exit ramp and making a quick right turn. By the time Jupe reached the top of the ramp the van had disappeared in traffic. His shoulders slumped as the others joined him. "Anybody get the license plate?" he asked.

"License plate! Are you kidding?" Pete said.

"If I'd stood still, I might have it printed on me now," Bob added.

"I didn't get the number either," Jupe admitted. "Or a look at the driver. Did we notice *anything*?"

"The van was a dark color. Gray, I think," said Bob.

"Black," Pete insisted.

Jupe shook his head. "I thought more like dark green."

"And one headlight was out," Pete said.

"Right. So we've got a dark Cyclops van. There should be only a few thousand like it in Los Angeles." Jupe sighed. "No problem at all."

"We've got a more immediate problem," Bob announced.

Pete and Jupe braced themselves. "What now?"

"Did either of you guys bring the key to our room?

When the door shut behind us, it automatically locked."

Jupe looked down at his pajamas, then at his friends' sleeping gear. Pete was in running shorts, Bob in drawstring sweatpants. "You mean we'll have to go to the registration desk and ask for a key—dressed like this? If word of this gets out, everyone will be *sure* we're the Three Stooges."

He stepped onto the sidewalk and made a left toward the front of the building. "Come on. We might as well enjoy a walk in the evening air. Besides, the front door is closer to the reception desk."

The wall rising beside them was solid concrete, but it soon turned into glass panels that dipped in, making room for a little garden and a side entrance to the hotel.

"Maybe we can sneak in through here," Pete suggested, stepping past a royal palm.

In the shadows under the tree something moved and groaned. The Investigators realized it was a human figure pulling itself up, a figure with a thin, angry face—Steve Tresh!

"What happened to *you*?" Jupe gasped.

Tresh had a swollen lip, bruises, and a definite mouse growing under one eye. He started to frown, then winced at the pain in his lip.

"I don't know what happened. I got tired of the noise in there and stepped outside. Next thing I know, somebody's jumping me." Tresh stood up, moving very slowly and carefully. "He worked me over pretty well. I never got a good look at the guy's face. But I have an idea who did this."

"Who?" Bob asked.

"Who was the last guy to take a swing at me?" Tresh asked, heading for the hotel entrance. "Leo Rottweiler."

Tresh went through the door, with the Investigators right behind. The artist was too upset to notice the guys' sleeping gear. Bob turned toward the reception desk, but Jupe shook his head. "Forget the keys."

Instead they followed Tresh across the lobby, their eyes straight ahead, trying to ignore the pointing and laughing. Jupe could see the red rising in Pete's ears. At least the elevator was right there. They stepped aboard and Tresh pressed three.

"Most of the pros and convention celebs are on the lower floors," Tresh explained as the elevator headed up. "I happened to hear that Rottweiler has room 335. We're going to pay him a little visit."

He marched down the hallway with the guys trailing after him and began pounding on the door to room 335. Leo Rottweiler answered it. His tie was loosened, but he was still in his suit.

Tresh grabbed him by the throat and started shaking him. "You didn't think you were going to get away with this, did you?" he yelled.

"Tresh, what are you doing?" cried Rottweiler. Confused voices came from inside the room as the Investigators tried to disentangle Tresh from the paunchy editor. They looked up to see Axel Griswold rushing toward them. Behind him were a bunch of comics people with glasses in their hands.

"What am I doing?" Tresh asked, lunging at Rottweiler again. "I'm going to rearrange your face, the way you tried to do mine."

"Why—why—what are you talking about?" Rottweiler stammered.

"Don't play innocent," Tresh shouted at him. "You jumped me outside."

"When did this happen?" Griswold wanted to know.

"It was only a few minutes ago. Ask him!"

But Griswold was shaking his head.

"No way," he said. "The party came up here to Leo's room a while ago. He couldn't have left—he's the host."

"Difficult, but not impossible," Jupe said.

"Maybe," Griswold said. "But I can personally vouch for the last half hour." He pointed at a large couch in the middle of the suite. "Leo and I were sitting over there talking."

He looked at Jupe right in the eyes. "And I think I'd have noticed if he left to beat Steve up."

9

Different Strokes

THE NEXT MORNING JUPE AWOKE EARLY. FROM THE SOUNDS of regular breathing around him, he realized Bob and Pete were still sleeping. He slipped out of bed carefully, without waking them. He dug a pair of swimming trunks out of his bag and put them on with a baggy shirt. Then he tiptoed toward the door—after making sure he had the key.

Jupe had decided that the pool would be the best place to do some thinking about the case. While he floated in the water, he could let his mind drift through all the facts and opinions they'd collected. Each time they made a step forward, the case became more confusing.

For instance, meeting Steve Tresh up close had changed the artist's "angry man" image. Yes, he had been angry, but he'd also shown a sense of humor. Jupe found it hard to imagine him as a thief.

Not only that, it was impossible for Tresh to have been the midnight visitor who broke into the Investigators' room. The guys had all agreed last night that the fight in the darkness could never have done that much damage to Tresh. They just hadn't been swinging hard enough to make him look like a human punching bag. So where had Tresh gotten those bruises?

Could he have beaten himself up to divert suspicion? That didn't make sense. Tresh wouldn't have had enough time between the disappearance of the van and his discovery by the Investigators.

For a second Jupe smiled at the ridiculous picture of Tresh ramming his head against the windshield to simulate injuries while deciding where to ditch the van. *That* theory wouldn't work. And somehow he didn't see Tresh as somebody who'd play for the sympathy vote.

Okay. So who beat up Tresh, and why? Did the beating tie in with the theft of the comics? Tresh was still the main robbery suspect. But the beating said somebody else was involved. It looked like they were stuck with a whole new mystery.

Jupe took the elevator downstairs. As he cut through the lobby on his way to the pool, he heard his name being called. He turned to see Axel Griswold hustling over to him.

"You're up early," the convention boss said.

"So are you," Jupe replied. "Especially after that late-night party."

"I don't have a choice," Griswold responded with a smile. "The earlier you start to work on conventions, the more disasters you get to find. Besides, I should count myself lucky. I managed to get *some* rest. There are red-eyed guys in the Gold Room who've spent the last twenty hours watching *Rock Asteroid*. When you come to a convention, you kiss sleep good-bye."

Actually, Griswold didn't seem to have missed much sleep. He was wearing fresh jeans and a new InterComiCon T-shirt. With his clipboard under his arm, he looked bright-eyed and ready for anything.

Jupe was sure he himself looked tired and grumpy, if not downright surly.

"How are you coming along with your case?" Griswold asked.

"We're still digging, and we keep coming up with puzzling things. I suppose you've guessed that Steve Tresh is a pretty strong suspect, especially since you knocked a hole in his alibi. But if he's the thief, why did somebody trash his room? And why was he beaten up?"

Griswold nodded, looking interested. "And what answers have you come up with?"

"None, so far. But all of a sudden someone seems determined to make Tresh's life miserable. That started me wondering if we haven't gotten things mixed around somewhere. Certainly Tresh comes off looking more like a victim than a crook."

As usual, Griswold glanced at his watch. "Thanks for sharing your thoughts with me," he said, heading off. Then he turned back, an expression of concern on his face. "You realize, though, there is another explanation for what's been happening to Tresh."

"What's that?" asked Jupe.

"The old-fashioned phrase is 'a falling-out among thieves.' "

◆　　◆　　◆

Chewing over those last words, Jupe was not in a good mood when he reached the pool. He dove in and started doing laps back and forth.

Exercise was never Jupe's thing. But he did enjoy swimming, with his powerful legs churning up the water and sliding him along. He swam the way he solved cases—slowly and methodically.

He broke into a powerful crawl, leaving his body on autopilot as he tried to fit the pieces of the case together. Somebody had attacked Steve Tresh. Someone had also attacked Pete in Tresh's room. And then there was the someone who had punched out all the Investigators last night. Not to mention the someone in the Crimson Phantom costume who stole the comics. Did all those someones add up to the same person?

Pete hadn't gotten a look at his attacker's face because of the frog mask, but he had seen a lot of muscle. That didn't match the looks of any of the theft suspects. Tresh was tall and lean, Carne was fat, Rottweiler had a potbelly—and Rainey Fields didn't fit the description at all.

So either the thief was somebody they didn't know about, or there was more than one person involved. As Jupe started examining possible combinations, he heard a splash behind him. He turned to get a blurry glimpse of a girl in a red tank suit coming up from a dive. Short brown hair was plastered around the sides of her face as she started swimming on a course parallel to his. Jupe continued on his way—*stroke-kick, stroke-kick*.

The girl in red soon caught up with him, then passed. By the time Jupe reached the far end of the pool, she was already on her return—the backstroke this time instead of the crawl.

As Jupe swam, he sneaked a peek over at the girl. She was pretty, tanned, and obviously enjoying herself. He'd barely reached the middle of the pool before she was coming back at him again.

Jupe stolidly kept up the same pace as the girl kept zipping back and forth. He felt like an old barge laboring its way along while some sleek hydrofoil sliced through the water past him. But Jupe knew better than to try to make a race of it. This kid definitely had him outclassed.

He outlasted her, though. After maybe twenty laps (to about a dozen of Jupe's) the girl swam to the side of the pool. Jupe found himself watching as she pulled herself out of the water, brushing back her hair with a quick gesture. Definitely gorgeous. And young. A teenager.

Treading water in the middle of the pool, Jupe watched her go over to one of the lounge chairs and pick up a towel. A beach bag lay under the chair. Obviously she'd staked her claim before she dove in.

After a quick rubdown with the towel, the girl lay

back in the chair. Then she got up and turned the chair toward the sun.

The slight adjustment knocked one of the legs of the lounge chair against her bag. It fell on its side and spilled open. The girl never noticed as she plopped back in the chair.

Jupe noticed, however. He stared at the bag—or rather, what was now spilling out of it.

Comic books.

Jupe was so surprised that he stopped moving for a second, and sank beneath the water.

Then he got his arms and legs in gear again and headed straight for the edge of the pool.

Even from the middle of the pool, Jupe had recognized the Investigators' business cards sticking out of those comics.

But all their comics with the cards were up in their room—they hadn't sold any.

That meant the comics in that bag had to be the ones stolen out of DeMento's hand in the smoke cloud!

What was this girl doing with them?

10

A Girl of Many Faces

JUPE BURST OUT OF THE WATER AND HAULED HIMSELF FROM the pool. The startled girl sat up in her lounger, staring at him.

He looked into her big hazel eyes and realized he knew his fellow swimmer. Only now she was a brunette instead of a blonde.

"Rainey!" he said furiously. "What are you doing here?"

Rainey Fields glanced around, a look of guilt on her face. "Oh, you're not going to tell, are you? I don't think anyone else has seen . . ."

Jupe looked down at the comics under the chair. "Why should I keep quiet about this?" he demanded.

But Rainey grabbed his hand. "*Please* don't tell," she begged him. "If this gets out, my mother will kill me!"

That was a line Jupe hadn't expected. He kept quiet as Rainey went on. "I thought that nobody would be around this early," she said. "So I figured it was worth the chance to take a swim. But if Mom finds out . . ."

Jupe blinked. Obviously there was a missed connection here. "What are you talking about?" he finally said.

"That stupid blond wig! I wanted to sneak in a quick swim, and I can't wear it in the pool. With my ordinary hair, a plain bathing suit, and no make-up, I didn't think anyone would recognize me. Guess I was wrong."

She sat, hugging herself tight. "I saw you after I was in the water. But you didn't say anything, so I figured I was okay. Just my luck, trying to fool a detective."

Rainey looked up at him pleadingly. "If Mom finds out I've been around out of costume, she'll positively freak! She'll swear I'll never get the job of modeling Stellara Stargirl. She'll—"

"Look," Jupiter cut her off. "I just want you to tell me what these are doing in here."

He picked up the beach bag with the comics and shoved it at her.

"What are you . . . ?" Then Rainey saw the comic books. "What are they doing in here?"

"Yeah, what?" Jupe replied grimly.

"They're not mine." Several emotions chased across Rainey's face. Puzzlement at the strange comics. Relief as she spotted the identifying cards. Then anger as she recognized Jupe's card. "These are yours! They have your cards in them. What are you scaring me for . . . ?"

Then came wide-eyed dismay. "Oh, no. I heard

that some of your comics had been stolen, too. These—these aren't the ones, are they?"

Jupe watched the whole performance. Either Rainey deserved an Oscar, or she was for real. He couldn't see how anyone could have faked those reactions. "Those *are* the missing comics," he said. "More than three hundred dollars' worth. Now, how did they get in your bag?"

Rainey leaned back, looking puzzled, but Jupe noticed her hands had clenched in her lap. "I have no idea," she admitted in a small voice.

Jupe could tell Rainey was beginning to realize her predicament. She was facing more trouble than a lecture from her mom about not wearing her costume. What would being caught with stolen property do to her career?

As she glanced up at him Rainey suddenly looked very vulnerable—and it wasn't just the lack of make-up. "This *is* your bag, isn't it?" Jupe asked a little more quietly.

Rummaging past the comics, Rainey came up with a comb and some sunglasses. "These are mine," she said miserably. "It must be my bag. But I swear I don't know where those comics came from."

"Did you talk to anybody this morning? Or maybe you left your bag out somewhere?" Jupe asked.

Rainey shook her head. "Uh-uh. *Not* seeing anybody was the whole idea. I didn't want anyone to recognize me. And my bag's been with me ever since I left my room."

She shrugged. "Except, of course, for the time I was in the water."

"Of course," Jupe echoed. His muscles tensed as he began to feel angry at himself.

It would be the easiest thing in the world to walk over to Rainey's bag and plant the comics in there. He scanned the quiet poolside. Nobody around—not even a lifeguard.

The only other possible witness was Jupe himself. And he'd been too busy looking at Rainey in her tank suit to notice anyone near the bag. The thief could have marched up with a brass band and planted anything he liked.

Rainey's voice broke into his thoughts. "I guess you want these back," she said timidly, holding out the comics. "They belong to you, after all. But why would anybody stick them in my bag?"

Her puzzled look changed to a grin. "It's like a corny movie where the master spy goofs up and gives the secret formula to the wrong person."

Jupe borrowed her towel to dry off before taking the comic books. Could that be it? Could this have been some kind of drop that went wrong?

"It strains credibility," Jupe said, riffling through the books. "I mean—"

She grinned. "You aren't so mad anymore. You're talking like usual now."

"Um," Jupe said unhappily. "These are all the ones we lost. Could this be the thief's way of dumping the books he didn't want? But why pick you?"

A thought suddenly struck Jupe. He'd already seen Rainey's mother in action. The woman was a born publicity hound. And what could be better publicity than for Rainey to find some of the stolen comics?

Of course, to do that, Ma Fields would have to get her hands on the stolen books. Or have stolen them herself.

He glanced down at Rainey, who looked up at him, all innocence. Certainly Rainey couldn't have done the job. He'd seen her and the Crimson Phantom together. But what about Mrs. Fields? She probably wouldn't even tell her daughter.

Jupe was about to ask a question when an angry voice hissed in his ear. "So this is where you are!"

He turned to find Mrs. Fields glaring past him at Rainey.

"What was the big idea of disappearing like that? I've been tracking you all over this hotel. And what do I find you doing? Sitting here—with one of those so-called detectives."

Jupe got a two-megaton glare from Rainey's mother as the girl quickly assembled her stuff.

"Sorry, Mom," Rainey said meekly.

Her mother thrust out a folding sun hat. "Now hide your hair under that and put on your sunglasses. Maybe no one will notice you."

She grabbed Rainey by the arm and started hauling her off. "Honestly, Rainey, I don't know what gets into you sometimes. I've managed to set up a major television spot for you today. You know we have to get ready. And what do you do? Go off to the pool to ruin your skin with sun and chlorine. Then, to top it off, you break our biggest rule!"

The woman whirled around to glare at Jupe again. "Young man," she said, "I sincerely hope that I don't hear any talk about my daughter's little secret. I'm sure you want to see her successful. If you do anything to hurt her chances, you'll have to deal with me."

Rainey stood behind her mother, looking deeply mortified. But as she was hauled off again, she managed a helpless little grin for Jupe.

As they rushed away Jupe noticed the way Mrs. Fields's clothes billowed as she moved. She was wearing a tentlike dress, almost like a robe.

As he watched the folded fabric move Jupe couldn't help thinking that the figure under the Crimson Phantom's robe didn't necessarily have to be a man.

11

Publicity Fiends

BOB AND PETE WERE ONLY HALF-AWAKE WHEN JUPE BURST back into room 316. But their eyes opened wide when they saw the comics in his hand.

"Where'd you get those?" Pete wanted to know, sitting up in bed.

"Through underwater surveillance," Jupe answered, deadpan. He was about to explain when the phone rang.

Pete picked it up with a "Who could this be?" expression on his face. Then his eyebrows went up as he listened. "For you, Bob. Your father."

"Hi, Dad. What's up?" Bob said after taking the phone. "Uh-huh. Yeah. Okay, I can take care of it." He hung up the phone, then turned to the guys. "Sax Sendler called. He's trying to book a band at a club in Van Nuys, and he needs to get a demo tape up there. Guess who's elected?"

"Look, I'll give you a lift," Pete offered.

"And I'll come along too." Jupe grinned. "Just as easy to tell my story on the way."

"Thanks, guys." Bob got back on the phone. He dialed Sax Sendler's number and told his boss he'd be arriving in about an hour.

Shortly afterward, they were hurrying down the hallway to the elevator. As they passed suite 314 the door opened. A guy with bleached spiky hair came out carrying a huge cardboard carton. "Okay, Axel," he said over his shoulder. "I'll take this stuff downstairs."

He was well behind them when the elevator arrived. "Hey, guys, can you hold that for me?" he called as the Investigators stepped inside.

"Sure." Pete pressed the OPEN button.

The guy hustled in. "Thanks a lot. I didn't want to be stuck holding these—whoa!"

His grip on the box slipped and it started to tip over. Jupe grabbed the box to steady it. He found himself looking inside—at stack after stack of videotapes.

"Thanks again," the young man said. "Could you press LOBBY for me?"

He got off the elevator, holding the box more carefully this time. Jupe, Bob, and Pete continued on down to the underground garage.

They made very good time on the freeways, arriving early at Sax Sendler's combination home/office in Rocky Beach. The talent agent came out the front door wearing his usual football jersey and squinting behind a pair of sunglasses. He handed a small package to Bob. "The guy who owns the club woke me from a sound sleep calling for this tape." He stifled a yawn. "It's unnatural for anyone in this business to be up at this hour."

He smiled as the Investigators each stifled yawns in reply. "Looks like you guys agree. Anyway, the address is on the package, and it shouldn't take you too long. I wouldn't have asked, but it's important."

"That's okay," Pete said. "We weren't doing anything."

"Much," Jupe added under his breath.

They delivered the tape with no problem, but as they drove back to L.A. along the San Diego Freeway they found themselves stuck in traffic.

Pete left the freeway, taking Sepulveda Boulevard as an alternate route. Passing through Santa Monica, he changed the route again, turning onto Pico.

"Don't look now, but I think Pete is taking us somewhere," Bob said.

"Since we were so close, I wanted to take another look at Madman Dan's," Pete admitted. "Something we saw last night has been nagging at me."

They drove along the boulevard until they were passing the comic shop. "There, about halfway down the block," Pete said.

He pulled up beside a battered green van—the same van DeMento had used to bring his comics to the convention the day before. "When we nearly got run down last night, we all thought the van was a different color," Pete said. "Jupe said it was green—and that started me thinking."

"There are lots of green vans in L.A.," Jupe said.

"But we have one easy way of checking." Pete jumped out of the car and ran around to the front of the van. He nodded grimly. "One headlight is cracked. We've found our Cyclops."

The rest of the ride back was a long, puzzled discussion. "If the van that nearly creamed us is DeMento's, that means he had to be the one who broke into our room," Bob said. "Why'd he do that? We're working for him, aren't we?"

"Maybe we're only providing a cover for him," Jupe said.

Bob gave him a sharp look. "You mean he's the one who stole the comics—and he hired three dumb teenagers to make himself look innocent." He nodded. "And he has a perfect motive—publicity."

"Everybody in the convention must have heard about the robbery at Madman Dan's stall," Jupe agreed. "I'll bet they all went over there to check it out."

Pete shook his head in admiration. "Well, he was ready for them. We saw all the extra stock he moved in yesterday." Then he frowned. "But we saw him there during the robbery. he couldn't have been the Crimson Phantom."

"No, but his assistant could," Jupe pointed out. "DeMento sent him away. A little while later the Crimson Phantom shows up to steal those books."

"That wraps it up nice and neat," said Pete. "Just one question: Can you accuse someone of stealing his own stuff?"

Bob shrugged. "I wouldn't bother. Why give him any more free publicity?" A wicked grin spread across his face. "If we really want to rattle his cage, let's show him the comics that mysteriously turned up again."

Jupe laughed, then got serious. "It might be a good idea. Depending on how he reacts, we can decide if he *is* the thief or whether we continue looking. Why don't we get the comics and bring them to the convention floor?"

They reached the hotel and headed back to their room. This time as they passed suite 314, Axel Griswold himself came out. "I've been looking for you guys! Is it true? I keep hearing that Rainey Fields found the stolen comics."

"Some of them—the ones that belonged to us." Jupe couldn't help grinning at the question. Ma Fields' publicity machine had to be running on overdrive!

As if reading Jupe's mind, Griswold shook his head. "Rainey's mother has been talking of nothing else. Her little TV spot has become a big deal now. By the way, she was looking for you. She wants to borrow the comics so Rainey can hold them for the camera."

He snickered. "There'll be a few news people there, but she's treating the whole thing like a remake of *Gone with the Wind*."

"Do you think she's going to burn down the hotel for the grand finale?" Jupe asked.

"Maybe that's the threat she used to twist the manager's arm." Griswold leaned forward. "I don't know how she did it, but she arranged for a special elevator for her daughter, complete with uniformed bellhop. Rainey will ride down to her audience in style."

He looked up suddenly. "There she is," he said. "Just think—she came to this convention a Stargirl, but she'll be leaving a star."

Jupe saw Rainey pass by, heading for the elevator. The tall girl was back in her Stellara Stargirl costume. When she saw Jupe, she gave him a nervous little smile. To Jupe's eyes it looked as though Rainey were fighting a major case of stage fright. He also noticed she was alone.

"I guess Mom is downstairs priming all the reporters," Griswold said. "Well, thanks, guys. At least now I know she isn't telling outright lies."

He went back into his room, leaving behind a ripe smell of sour grapes. Why? Jupe wondered. Isn't this great publicity for the convention?

"Do you guys mind if we lend Rainey the comics for this TV thing?" he asked abruptly.

Pete shrugged.

"Sure, why not?" said Bob.

They went into their room, grabbed the pile of comics, then headed back to the elevator.

Rainey was a solitary figure in front of her private elevator. She carefully adjusted her blue cape. She kept staring at the doors as if she could will them to open for her ride to fame. Or was she hoping they'd stay shut?

Jupe was about ten feet from her when the elevator chimes rang out.

"Hey, Rainey," he called, holding up the comics he'd gotten for her.

She turned around, glad to see a friendly face.

That was why she didn't notice anything was wrong with the elevator.

Instead of the usual brightly lit cab, the doors had opened on darkness.

And the arms that reached out to grab Rainey weren't in any bellhop's uniform.

12

Jupe to the Rescue

JUPE TORE TOWARD THE ELEVATOR WITH PETE AND BOB AT his heels. They got there just as the doors closed in their faces. The solid steel cut off Rainey's voice in midscream.

Still clutching the comics in his hands, Jupe whipped around, white-faced. "Come on!"

He ran to the service stairs they'd used on their wild chase of last night's intruder. Tearing open the door, he plunged down the steps at top speed.

Jupe thought he'd never moved so fast. Even Pete was having a tough time keeping up with him. And Bob made a poor third.

Jupe's legs began to ache as he whirled around another landing. Can we catch up with Rainey? he wondered. She's in a high-speed elevator.

But he kept moving as fast as he could, jumping the stairs two and three at a time.

They reached the lobby floor, but Jupe kept going downward. No way was the kidnapper going to come out of the elevator in front of all those TV cameras.

Nor could he risk taking the elevator to one of the other floors. Someone might be standing at the elevator bank, waiting for a ride.

No, the safest place for this guy to head was the nice quiet parking garage. Just the place to bring a struggling victim.

Jupe flew down the last flight of stairs. Just like the night before he hit the panic bar on the door. This time, however, he was moving so fast the door swung as if it had been blasted open.

Jupe *had* to move fast. If that guy got Rainey into a car before they reached him . . .

He dashed for the elevator bank. The sounds of scuffling and muffled screams were almost welcome. They meant Rainey was still there—and still fighting.

"C'mon, kid, stop being stupid. I don't want to hurt you. Just tell me where you hid my stuff, and there'll be no problems."

That voice was familiar. And as he came round in front of the elevators Jupe saw he was right. Dragging Rainey along in a choke hold was Dan DeMento.

A flutter of paper in the face was the first hint to DeMento that he had company. It was the fistful of comics Jupe still held in his hand.

Jupe couldn't have hoped for a more successful diversion. DeMento jumped, then half-turned in surprise. His arm loosened its hold around Rainey's neck.

That was all Jupe needed. He literally tore De-Mento away from the girl, hurling him into a concrete wall. The comics dealer hit the wall with a thud and wavered for a second, stunned.

Rainey tottered toward Jupe, about to fall.

Jupe turned and reached out to catch her. DeMento jumped at him. Jupe met the attack with a straight-arm blow that sent DeMento bouncing back to the wall.

Bob caught the swaying Rainey, while Pete moved in to help Jupe finish the job of subduing DeMento. In seconds they had him pinned to the wall.

"Not so easy when you have to fight guys instead of a girl, is it?" Jupe yelled in the comic dealer's face.

He forced his anger back, which wasn't so easy. Especially when he heard Rainey saying in a quavery voice, "Oh, Bob, you saved me!"

About the most serious thing Bob had saved her from was a scraped knee. But this wasn't the time to tell Rainey that. She was still too shaken up by the attack.

"You're okay now," Jupe told Rainey. "We'll take care of that creep."

Rainey gradually calmed down. Then a thought suddenly struck her. "They're waiting for me upstairs!" she exclaimed. "Mom will kill—"

Abruptly she went down on one knee, picking up the comics that Jupe had thrown. She glanced over at Jupe, then looked back at the floor. "Thank you, guys. All of you." She took a deep breath, then asked Bob, "Do I look all right? I've got to go up."

"You look fine," Bob assured her. "Go on."

"I don't think I'll mention what happened down here," Rainey said. "I'll talk to you about it later."

Jupe heard her get back in the elevator. He couldn't bear to look. How typical. After all his worrying, his fighting—*Bob* becomes her hero.

Once again Jupe had to swallow his anger. Then he thought of a more constructive use for it. There was a lot to be shaken out of Dan DeMento.

"We've got to stop meeting like this," Bob said to DeMento.

"Wha—what do you mean?" DeMento's hair was wilder than ever. He shook his head, still trying to get over being knocked around.

"You mean you've forgotten all about last night?" Jupe asked. "When you nearly ran all three of us down?"

"With your nice green van," Pete added, taking Jupe's cue. "The one with the broken headlight."

"I didn't mean to—I mean . . ."

"What *do* you mean?" Jupe pressed DeMento hard. "Burglary, trying to kill us, kidnapping that girl . . ."

"It wasn't that way at all!" DeMento insisted, his voice shaking. "I heard that the girl in the gold outfit had found the stolen comics. Then the story changed—she'd only found *your* comics. That sounded fishy to me."

He squinted angrily. "I saw her by my stall right before the comics got stolen. Now she was suddenly 'finding' some of them. I figured she must have them all. And I wanted to get her alone, to find out where she'd hidden them. So I got rid of the bellhop for a minute and borrowed his elevator."

For a horrible second Jupe wondered if they had just let the real thief make her escape on the elevator. No. Rainey's surprise and shock at finding the books had been genuine. "You picked the wrong person, DeMento. I was there when she found the comics. Somebody had slipped them into her bag."

"I had to do *something!*" For a moment Madman Dan looked like a real madman as he pleaded with Jupe. "I've been going nuts ever since that guy ripped me off. And it didn't look like you guys were coming up with much. So I started poking around on my own. That's why I went to that room last night."

"You wanted to search *our* room?" Pete asked.

"I didn't even know you guys were in there. All I knew was that it was connected to 314, and I wanted to get into the suite to search—"

"Axel Griswold?" Bob's voice was disbelieving.

"Axel Griswold's *stock.*" Jupe tapped his forehead with his fist. "That guy with the box of videotapes who came out of Griswold's room this morning. I should have remembered where I'd seen him. He was the one selling the hot tapes at the Kamikaze Komics stall."

Jupe looked at Dan DeMento, who had calmed down a little when he saw he wasn't about to be lynched.

"What's the connection between Griswold and Kamikaze Komics?" Jupe asked.

"He owns the place," Madman Dan answered

promptly. "Didn't you know? That's how he got into running these conventions. He's been a comics dealer for years."

"A comics dealer for years," Jupe repeated, trying to fit this new information in with all the rest they'd gathered.

One thing was certain, at least. Dan DeMento could not be the thief.

The robbery itself, even the break-in at the Investigators' room, could be explained as publicity gimmicks. But kidnapping a girl was not the kind of publicity a sane person would want.

Jupe sighed. He'd just lost a suspect. And he found himself back at square one again.

There was one question he wanted to ask DeMento, though.

"When we saw you with that replacement issue of *Fan Fun*, the price sticker said two hundred and fifty dollars. Yet when Leo Rottweiler tried to buy the one that was stolen, you quoted six hundred dollars and he actually considered paying it. What makes that copy so valuable?"

A crafty smirk spread over Dan DeMento's face. "It was autographed by Steve Tresh," he explained. "A real collector's item. A Steve Tresh original."

13

Rainey Shows Her Hand

"AUTOGRAPHED?" JUPE SAID. "I DON'T COLLECT COMICS, and even I know Steve Tresh doesn't sign any Crimson Phantom stuff. Frank Carne told me the whole story. I even saw Tresh refusing to sign art for the fans."

"You're absolutely right," DeMento said, his smirk growing bigger under his unruly mustache. "But this is *Fan Fun*—and the *Gray* Phantom. It came out long before *The Crimson Phantom*. I figure Tresh must have autographed the book before all the trouble began. And it was all mine."

The smirk abruptly disappeared. "It *was* all mine. Until some creep stole it."

Jupe frowned in thought. "You never got a chance to show that book to Tresh, did you?"

Madman Dan shook his head. "I didn't even meet him until after the book was stolen. And instead of talking about the book, I wound up going after Frank Carne."

He looked at the Three Investigators and cleared his

throat. "Uh, guys, what are you going to do about me?"

"Oh, you mean about last night?" Jupe asked. "That little business of breaking and entering, assault, and reckless endangerment?"

"Yeah." DeMento was really sweating now. "That business."

Jupe shrugged. "The only thing we could go to the police and prove is a traffic violation. You should get your headlight fixed."

DeMento relaxed a little.

Then Bob spoke up. "But Rainey Fields will have to make up her own mind about what happened today. She said she wanted to talk with us about it. Maybe you should be deciding what *you'll* say."

That's right, Jupe thought. Rainey would be coming back to talk to them.

"I really should be heading upstairs to my stall," DeMento said. He gave them a wry smile. "You know where to find me. Maybe you could bring her over. Whatever happens, I should give her an explanation— and an apology."

"Sounds good to me," Pete said, pushing the elevator button. "So, what do we do next?"

"Let's try and find Steve Tresh," Jupe said promptly. "I want to talk about autographs."

They rode up to the lobby together and headed for the main conference room. There was a small line of stragglers at the table by the entrance getting hand stamps from the girl with the two-toned hair.

DeMento hurried off toward his stall. As Bob, Pete, and Jupe tried to enter, however, the husky security guard blocked their path. "Sorry, guys, that stamp looks awful faded."

He peered at the backs of their hands and gave them his chip-toothed grin. "Just like I thought. Yesterday's stamp. Nice try, guys."

Jupe reached for his wallet. "I knew there was something else we were supposed to do this morning."

A few moments later, with INTERCOMICON—DAY 2 stamped on their hands, the Investigators were plowing through the crowd on the convention floor.

"Next stop, Steve Tresh," Pete said, looking around. "Where do you think we'll find him?"

"I think our first shot should be the artists' tables," Jupe suggested. "If he's not there, at least someone might be able to tell us where he went."

Tresh's seat was empty, and there were no hopeful fans around his table. Worse still, none of the artists knew where he was. "He left a while ago," said an older man, carefully inking in a pencil sketch of Wacky Wodent. "Didn't say anything. Just went."

"Any other ideas?" Bob asked Jupe.

"When in doubt, try the hotel reception desk," Jupe answered.

"No, I'm afraid Mr. Tresh can't be reached," the reception clerk told Jupe. "He's in an important meeting."

"Did he say when he'd be available?" Jupe asked.

"Sometime this afternoon," she said.

"Could I leave a message for him?" Jupe took a pen and paper from the clerk, scribbled a brief note, and handed it back to her. "I asked him to meet us at DeMento's stall," he told the others.

"Well, now we know where we'll spend the afternoon," Pete responded.

Madman Dan looked nervous when he saw the Investigators coming toward him. "Did you talk to the girl yet?" he asked.

He relaxed a bit when Jupe explained what they were doing there. "Sure. Anything I can do to help. I suppose you want Tresh to talk to me anyway."

Just then a kid came staggering up. He was almost invisible behind a huge cardboard carton, which was about three times the size of the comic box the Investigators had left in their room. "Excuse me, guys," DeMento said. "This looks like business."

The kid dropped his box to the floor and peered up at Madman Dan suspiciously. "Think we can do a trade?" he whined, leaning heavily against the table. "I'm trying to get *Slime Man* Number One. I've got Number One and Number Two of *The Outrageous Ooze*."

DeMento nodded. "Sounds like a pretty fair trade."

He turned to the back rack of the stall and reached for *Slime Man*.

At the same time, the kid hoisted the box up and dropped it sharply on the edge of the table.

DeMento was just in the act of handing over the comic. "Here you—watch out!" The table collapsed.

"Gosh, I'm sorry. Let me help clean up." The kid got down on his knees, picking up the comics that had fallen off the table. DeMento and his assistant were busy getting the folding table to stand up again.

The kid left the comics in a big pile, then started pushing his box away.

Madman Dan planted a foot in his way. "Just a second," he said, pulling the carton open. He quickly plucked out a comic. "Here's my copy of *Slime Man*. I wonder how it got in there?" He shook the comic in the kid's face. "No deal, kid. Beat it, and don't come back."

The kid disappeared quickly, considering the size of the box he had to lug away.

Madman Dan watched him go, shaking his head. "He's probably got a few more of my comics in there. That's why I keep the money stuff in the back—and only cheapies on the front table."

He laughed. "And Frank Carne thinks *I'm* a crook."

The mention of Frank Carne's name sparked a thought in Jupe's mind. This little sideshow had just eliminated Frank the Crank as a suspect. While the Crimson Phantom's billowing robe might have concealed his identity, there was no way a person of his bulk could have vaulted over the table. Not without bringing it to the floor. But could the Phantom have been Mrs. Fields?

"Hi, guys."

Jupe turned to see Rainey Fields holding out a stack

of comic books. "I saw you over here and figured I should return these," she said.

"Uh—thanks." Jupe tucked the pile under his arm, a little embarrassed to think he'd just been suspecting Rainey's mother. "How did your interviews go?"

"Fine. Mom told me that I was finally learning showmanship—making them wait a minute before making my entrance. If she knew the *real* reason . . ." She shuddered, her eyes flicking over to Dan De-Mento. "I guess it's time to talk."

DeMento kept nervously stacking and restacking comics. "I want to say I'm sorry," he began. "I made a big mistake."

By the time Madman Dan had finished his explanation, Rainey had accepted his apology. Then she turned to Jupe. "I owe *you* an apology, too."

Jupe stared in surprise as she went on. "You were the one who jumped in and saved me—and I didn't really thank you." Her eyes shone. "I never saw anyone fight like that before."

"Oh, uh, yeah." Jupe could feel his face turning bright red as Rainey patted his hand.

"Thank you."

"Well, uh, why don't, uh . . ." Jupe couldn't understand it. All of a sudden his tongue felt glued to the roof of his mouth. He could feel Pete and Bob staring at him.

Finally he took Rainey by the arm and led her a few steps away. "Why don't we go out and have lunch?" Amazing. The words came out sounding halfway normal.

"Okay." Rainey leaned forward, a conspiratorial glint in her eyes. "I'll meet you in the garden by the side entrance—twenty minutes."

Then she was gone.

Jupe could not believe his luck. He turned back to his friends. "I'm having lunch with Rainey. You guys don't mind, do you?"

"Oh, no." Bob shook his head. "And even if I did, you'd probably smooth-talk me into changing my mind."

"Right," said Pete. "I've got to remember that line. 'Well, uh, why don't, uh. . . .' "

"Thanks, guys," Jupe muttered as he headed for their room to drop off the comics and neaten up. "Thanks a lot."

Jupe didn't know what to expect as he waited in the garden. What he got was Rainey in shorts and a T-shirt, with her short brown hair. She looked normal, everyday—and gorgeous.

"Is this your secret identity?" he asked.

Rainey grinned. "You've got it." She linked her arm through his and led him onto the sidewalk. She was a bit taller than Jupe's 5 feet 8¾ inches, but Jupe didn't even care.

"I'm glad for a chance to get out of that crazy costume," Rainey went on. "And I know this great place nearby—burgers and salads and stuff. Where nobody cares about Stellara Stargirl."

The restaurant was light and airy, with lots of glass, lots of plants—and lots of alfalfa sprouts, as Jupe quickly found out. Rainey ordered the same salad as Jupe, eating it with much more enjoyment than he did.

But then she hadn't had to live on alfalfa sprouts for two weeks. When he'd read the book on this diet, it had seemed like an easy way to lose weight. Now he was getting awfully tired of sprouts—and he was about twenty-five miles behind on his walking.

Rainey had the Investigators' card out and was reading it. "You really investigate crimes?" she said.

He shrugged. "We've done it for years."

"And you're the founder. The other two guys are your associates." She looked up at him.

"That is what it says on the card." A big clump of sprouts dropped from Jupe's fork onto the table. He quickly shoved it under his plate. Oh, great, he thought. Now that I've got my mouth working, my hands begin to shake.

"It must be great to have a team like that. Your big friend—Pete? He looks pretty strong."

Jupe nodded. "Yeah. He's a real jock."

Rainey leaned forward on the table. "And your other friend—Bob. What's he like?"

Another forkful of sprouts landed on the table. Jupe sighed. He should have seen this coming.

For the rest of the lunch Jupe talked about some of the criminals they'd put away—and Bob. Weird clues they'd discovered—and Bob. Tough cases they'd cracked—and, of course, Bob. Jupe only managed to steer the conversation away from Bob for a few brief minutes, when he got Rainey to talk about herself.

"Why do you go around in that crazy costume?" he asked.

"It's kind of hard to explain," Rainey said. "I've always liked comics. Mom didn't really appreciate that—until she saw Stellara Stargirl and figured this could get me started as a model."

"Is that what you want to do?"

"Nah." Rainey laughed. "I want to be a comic artist."

Jupe started laughing too. "Drawing Slime Man?"

"Not exactly. But it might be fun to have a girl drawing Stellara Stargirl."

After that, Jupe couldn't think of anything else to say. When the time came to pay for lunch, he was almost glad.

They were back in the garden by the hotel's side entrance. "Thanks. I had a nice time," Rainey told him.

"Yeah, uh, nice." Jupe's tongue seemed to have gotten itself disconnected again. He took a step forward.

"I'll see you around. Will you be staying through tomorrow?" As she spoke Rainey stuck out her hand.

Jupe stared at her hand. Oh, no. She was going to shake hands. A humiliating lunch and a good-bye *handshake*.

"I don't know how long we'll be here. Until we

clear up this case." Jupe decided he might as well get the handshake over with. He took her hand. "Take it easy . . . Hey!"

"What?" Rainey tried to pull her hand away, but Jupe wouldn't let go. He kept turning their right hands back and forth, staring at the black letters stamped on the back.

"Jupe," she said, "what are you doing?"

"Realizing something that I should have noticed a long time ago."

"Something you saw at the robbery?"

He patted the back of her hand. "Something I *didn't* see. When the Crimson Phantom dropped those smoke bombs, I saw the backs of both his hands."

"So?" Rainey said.

"So," Jupe answered, "neither of them was stamped."

14

A Dead Deal

STILL HOLDING RAINEY'S HAND, JUPE RUSHED TOWARD THE door. "We've got to see the guys and let them know about this."

"Hold it!" Rainey finally yanked her hand free. "I can't go on the convention floor looking like this. Somebody might recognize me. And if that happens, my mom—"

"Will kill you," Jupe finished for her.

"Besides, what's so important about our hands?" she asked.

"It proves the robbery was an inside job," Jupe explained. "You, me, the dealers—*anybody* who came into the convention had to get their hands stamped—an indelible ticket we had to show at the door. But the person who dropped those smoke bombs had clean hands. No stamp. How did he get in? He couldn't—unless he was working here."

"I see what you mean." Rainey hesitated, looking across the lobby toward the elevator bank. "Look, I want to help on this case, if I can. After all, I'm involved now. Let me go upstairs and get back into costume. I'll meet you at Madman Dan's booth."

"Want me to walk you to your room?" Jupe asked.

Rainey grinned. "No. I think I'll be safe on the elevator this time."

Jupe headed back to the main conference room, presenting his hand with a flourish to the gorilla security guard. He made his way through the crowd to Madman Dan's stall. Standing in front of it were Bob and Pete.

"Did Stellara Stargirl take you over to the next galaxy for lunch?" Pete asked.

"Is there anything you want to tell us?" Bob's voice sounded serious, but he kept waggling his eyebrows at Jupe. "Have you learned anything new about life?"

"I discovered a clue while you guys were thinking up gags," Jupe said. "Has Steve Tresh showed up yet?"

"Somebody mention my name?" asked Steve Tresh as he walked up to the stall. "Good timing," the sandy-haired artist said with a smile. "I just got here myself, and I'm ready for a celebration." He tapped the pocket of his jacket. "In here is a contract signed with an independent distributor. My new comic will be shipped nationwide as soon as it gets off the press."

"Which distributor?" Dan DeMento asked.

"Ned Root. He was in town for the convention, so we did our business right in his suite. Hush-hush stuff. I had to sneak away for our meetings."

"Is that where you were when Dan got robbed?" Jupe asked.

Tresh nodded. "After I'd made my first presentation to Ned, I came down to the convention floor and found it full of smoke. I guess you guys know the rest."

"Did anyone know about your negotiations?"

"Nobody. Like I said. I wasn't going to ruin the *Major Mayhem* deal by blabbing around about it."

"*Major Mayhem?*" DeMento broke in, his mustache quivering. "What kind of a hero is he? A wrestler? A GI? A mercenary? A rock star?"

Tresh gave him a sly smile. "You'll just have to buy the first issue and see." He looked at Jupe. "Why did you ask if anyone knew about the negotiations?"

Jupe lowered his voice. "I've been thinking about what's happened to you—the destruction of your artwork and the attack last night. Whoever did it to you obviously didn't know you had a strong reason to stick around."

Bob leaned forward. "Jupe, this keeps getting heavier and heavier. You make it sound like somebody is trying to drive Steve away."

"That's exactly what I'm trying to say." Jupe looked at Tresh. "If you didn't have to stay for this distribution deal, would you have hung around?"

"No way—not even to make my speech," the artist admitted. "I was beginning to think Rottweiler had somehow gotten wind of the negotiations and was trying to wreck them. But you said—"

"The person *didn't* know about the impending deal," Jupe said. "Otherwise I expect Mr. Root would have been having problems too. The attacks were aimed directly at you, Steve, and I believe they're tied up somehow with that stolen copy of *Fan Fun*. They *have* to be."

He looked over at DeMento. "Why don't you ask him about that autograph?"

"Autograph?" Tresh looked wary. "I hope you're not going to ask me to sign some stupid piece of—"

"This is about something you already signed," DeMento said quickly.

"*May* have signed," Jupe added.

"What?" Tresh still looked suspicious.

"I've seen you refuse to autograph artwork from your Heroic Comics days," Jupe said. "I've even seen you burn it."

"Oh, you caught that little act, too." Now Tresh was becoming embarrassed. "I guess I got a little carried away there. But I think I had good reason. Heroic Comics, and especially Leo Rottweiler, gave me a really raw deal."

"We know," Jupe said. "Frank the Crank told us all about it."

The artist jammed his hands into his pockets. "Well, there's no way I'm going to help their business along by autographing my old artwork."

"You weren't always angry at Heroic Comics," DeMento pointed out. "How about the time before you quit? You must have autographed stuff then."

Tresh laughed. "Back then Heroic was giving me so much work doing art and scripts, I was too busy to sign my own name. Or too tired."

"And before that?" DeMento went on. "Your *Fan Fun* days."

"What? Oh, you mean the Gray Phantom story." Tresh shook his head. "I wasn't famous enough to sign autographs back then. Who cares about an unknown artist?"

"Well, maybe you forgot about it, but you must have signed one," DeMento insisted. "For your mother, or your girlfriend, a buddy . . . maybe someone you were working with."

"I think I would have remembered signing a Gray Phantom story." Tresh frowned. "What's this about?"

"I had a copy of *Fan Fun* with your autograph." Madman Dan was absolutely sure.

"You couldn't. I never signed any." Tresh sounded equally positive.

"Look, it was your name. Right across the splash page of your story."

Tresh's eyes narrowed. "If only I could see it."

"But of course you can't," Jupe said. "The robbery took care of that."

The artist turned to DeMento. "Do you remember what the autograph looked like?" he asked. "My signature has changed a lot from those days. We could tell if somebody copied an autograph from something more recent. Because I sure don't remember ever signing that book."

"Maybe it's one you don't want to remember," DeMento said. "Because the guy who sold it to me would certainly know your signature."

"Who was it?" Pete asked.

"Leo Rottweiler."

The Investigators stared at DeMento in disbelief.

"That snake!" Tresh burst out. "I wouldn't give him the time of day, much less an autograph."

"I thought it was something he had from when you were still friendly—when you were working together," DeMento said.

"Our working days were never exactly friendly." Tresh smiled bitterly. "He was the old pro, the big editor, and I was the kid starting out. He gave *me* an autograph once. When I left Heroic, I burned the dumb thing."

"So where did Rottweiler get the book?" asked Bob.

"I don't know," Tresh replied. "But it wasn't from me."

With a swirl of blue cape and a glitter of gold costume, Rainey rushed up. "Did I miss anything?"

"No," Jupe said. "You're just in time for the fireworks. We're going to have a chat with Leo Rottweiler."

"I'd like to punch him in the mouth," Tresh muttered.

"Well, I wouldn't hold you back," DeMento said to him. "He's responsible for the latest cute trick from Heroic. They're reprinting old issues of their successful books as Heroic Classics."

"You mean he's reprinting the stuff we used to read?" Pete said.

DeMento nodded. "Especially your stuff, Steve. Crimson Phantom Classics will take in big bucks. Of course," he went on bitterly, "it drives down the value of the original books. And I'm stuck with a bunch of them, taking a loss."

"Is that why you gave Rottweiler such a hard time when he tried to buy *Fan Fun* back?" Jupe asked.

"Yeah," said DeMento, smiling. "He pestered me for days, but I wouldn't give him the satisfaction."

"Well, gentlemen, let's see what Mr. Rottweiler has to say," said Jupe.

They reached the Heroic Comics area, which was set up for another press conference. Leo Rottweiler smiled at Rainey. His smile faded when he noticed who was following her.

"Tresh!" He gave the artist a thin smile. "Come to make more ridiculous accusations?"

"No, we've just come to ask a few questions." Jupe was the soul of courtesy. "We're all interested in that collector's item you were trying to buy back."

"Buy back? I don't know what you're talking about," the balding editor blustered, but his eyes began darting around nervously when he saw Dan DeMento.

"You know. That copy of *Fan Fun* Number One you tried to buy from Mr. DeMento here." Jupe went on as if Rottweiler had never spoken. "He told us that you were the one who originally sold it to him."

"What has that got to do with anything?" Two small red dots appeared over Rottweiler's cheeks. "I won't put up with another half-baked accusation!"

"Oh, we know you didn't *steal* the book," Jupe cut him off. "You were with Frank Carne outside the

Gold Room when the smoke bombs went off. What we wanted to know was why you were so anxious to buy the fanzine back."

"I, ah, got a much better offer for the book, and saw the chance to make a profit. Nothing wrong with that, is there?"

Jupe nodded. "But you couldn't make the deal, could you?"

"No." Rottweiler pointed a shaking finger at De-Mento. "Because *he* kept pushing the price impossibly high, until, ah, my prospective buyer cut it off."

"So who was the prospective buyer?" Pete asked.

Rottweiler licked his lips.

"It's a dead deal, Mr. Rottweiler," Bob spoke up. "Why don't you tell us who wanted it?"

"Kamikaze Komics." Rottweiler had a trapped look on his face as he answered.

"Where did you get the book in the first place?" Tresh asked. "I know it wasn't from me."

Rottweiler gave up completely. "Kamikaze Komics," he muttered.

"I don't think we have to disturb Mr. Rottweiler any more," Jupe said.

The group filed out of the stall.

"Very, *very* interesting," Jupe said. "An inside job. A store that sells a comic and suddenly wants it back. Things are finally coming together. A few more answers and we should have our thief." He smiled and sped up the aisle. "And I know just where to look."

15

Big Shop of Horrors

JUPE VEERED OFF TO THE LEFT SO SHARPLY THAT HE almost lost the rest of his parade in the crowd.

"Hold on. Where are we going?" Rainey asked as she caught up with him.

"Where all the problems in this convention seem to come from." He stopped across the aisle from the Kamikaze Komics stall.

There was no way the Investigators and their friends could get any closer. The crowd at the stall was the densest they'd seen that weekend—literally wall-to-wall bodies.

"You'd think they were giving out things for free," Bob said.

"They just about are," one red-faced, happy collector told him. "These tapes were going for thirty bucks yesterday. I got this for ten!"

"That's still much more than the tape is really worth," Jupe whispered. Yet he found himself intrigued. Why were they selling everything off?

He plunged into the crowd to find out. After several

minutes of dodging through wriggling bodies and thumping elbows, he reached the counter. The Kamikaze crew was really hopping, serving up comics and videotapes at real discounts. "Okay, sport, what are you looking for?" the blond spiky-haired guy asked Jupe.

"Um—*Stellara Stargirl*?" It was the first comic name to enter Jupe's mind.

"Good choice! We've got a special here, numbers one through five, all wrapped together. Usually fifty dollars"—he looked at Jupe appraisingly—"for you, fifteen."

Jupe had no choice but to shell out the money. As he did he looked at the guy's hands. No, he hadn't been the Crimson Phantom. His fingers were stubby, the nails bitten, and the stamp was prominent on the back of his hand.

Jupe's eyes flicked to the other salesmen's hands as his change was counted out. None fit the bill.

"There you go. Thanks!" The guy turned to one of the workers. "Hey, Jerry, we need some more of the special merchandise."

"This?" The guy pulled out another package of *Stellara Stargirl* comics. Jupe noticed that the cover price was ten bucks.

"No, stupid, the *special* merchandise. They'd better bring it over from the store. We've got some live ones here."

Jupe fought his way free of the mob scene and rejoined his group. Rainey began to laugh when she saw what he'd bought. "You can autograph them for me later," Jupe told her. "We have a little field trip now."

"Field trip? Where?" DeMento asked.

"Kamikaze Komics. They're selling a lot of this junk." Jupe waved his packaged set. "But they have some kind of special merchandise over at the store. I wonder if it's so special that they had to steal it back."

"And you want to see what's there. Well, I've got a van." Madman Dan shrugged his shoulders. "My assistant will just have to mind my stall until we get back."

"I'm coming too," Rainey announced. She looked down at her gold outfit. "But I don't think I'm dressed right . . ."

"Here." Tresh gave her his jacket. "We might need a superperson down in that neighborhood."

They went to the parking garage and took off— Tresh, Rainey, and Madman Dan in the green van, the Investigators in Pete's Impala.

"You're sure you know where this store is?" Jupe asked as they pulled up the ramp.

"DeMento said it was on Hollywood near Western," Pete answered. "He said we couldn't miss it."

He was right—they *couldn't* miss it. Kamikaze Komics had the ground floor of an old four-story building, but they'd painted the whole front into an ad for the store. Against a blinding yellow background flying superheroes battled Japanese Zeros. "Kamikaze Komics." Bob laughed. "What else?"

They parked, then gathered at the van to discuss strategy. "You know, I used to hang out here all the time when I started collecting comics," DeMento said. "They had the cheapest prices."

"And the lowest rent," Tresh added, looking around the shabby neighborhood.

"Back then," DeMento went on, "the basement of the shop sold secondhand paperbacks. Now it's used for storage. Whatever we're looking for should be down there." DeMento looked around the group. "I know where the cellar stairs are, but they'll stop us unless we have a distraction."

Rainey grinned and opened Steve Tresh's jacket. "I think I can take care of that."

Moments later they put their hastily developed plan into action. During the next five minutes Tresh, DeMento, and Jupe wandered in, acting like casual customers. Five minutes after that, Rainey was to follow. Bob and Pete would stay outside, ready to come in as reinforcements if anything went wrong.

Jupe had half-expected to find the same booming business he'd seen at the convention stall. But Kami-kaze Komics was like a ghost town—two bored-looking clerks and maybe four customers with their noses buried in the comics racks.

The dingy walls had once been much more densely stocked. Jupe could see clean squares in the dust where whole boxes had been removed. It's beginning to look like a going-out-of-business sale, he thought. But it seems to be happening awfully fast.

He glanced around and spotted DeMento. He was standing by a door in the rear of the store. The big clean-out had actually helped them. A lot of boxes had been cleared out of that area, opening it up. Jupe walked over, occasionally taking a look at a comic. Tresh worked his way over too.

Then the front door opened and Rainey walked in, her costume shining and a big grin on her face. She had the same effect she'd had at the convention. Every head turned toward her.

Except for Jupe, Tresh, and DeMento. Madman Dan eased open the basement door, and the three of them zipped down the stairs. A dusty forty-watt bulb hung over the stairway, casting a feeble glow.

Jupe looked for a light switch as he, DeMento, and Tresh reached the bottom. No luck. Not that there was so much to see in the dimness. Just a small pile of boxes and a big pile of disassembled machinery.

Jupe stared at the pieces. Somewhere he'd seen a machine like this. Where? Slowly the memory came together. The salvage yard. Uncle Titus coming back from a closed-down print shop. "You know what this is?" Jupe whispered. "An old offset printing press. But what were they printing?"

He stepped forward, and his toe hit a crumpled wad of paper. It skittered across the floor toward Tresh, who picked it up and straightened it out. "Hey, Dan," he said, "know what this is?"

The page was crudely printed in black and white. It looked like a collection of daily comic strips.

"Sure." DeMento peered at it. "In the early days they used to reprint newspaper comics into black-and-white yearly books. That page must be fifty years old."

"I think this is a newer reprint." Tresh pointed at the page. "This pulp paper should be yellow and brittle. It should have split when I unfolded it."

"Well, now we know what the 'specials' are," Jupe said. "Counterfeit comics."

"Yeah," said a voice from the doorway. "So now what do we do with you?"

They looked up the stairway. Three figures were silhouetted against the lights of the store. One stepped forward into the dim glow of the stair light. Jupe recognized him then—the beefy security guard from the convention entrance.

"I thought you guys would have gotten the hint when your big pal went flying without wings. But no, Fat Boy's got to go around asking questions, Skinny has to stick his nose where it's not wanted, and Big Guy's still leading with his chin." He grinned down at them, showing his chipped tooth. "I hope you're not thinking about hollering or anything. We just closed the store. And the walls here are pretty thick."

"Purvis," one of the store clerks said nervously, "what are we supposed to do?"

"Yeah, Purvis," Jupe asked. "What *are* you supposed to do? How'd you know we were here?"

"That dippy Rottfink guy came squealing to the boss that you'd been asking questions about us. He figured you'd be coming to the store." He grinned again. "And he sent me here to take care of you three."

He can't see us clearly in the dark, Jupe realized. He thinks DeMento and Tresh are Pete and Bob. "I bet you do a lot of 'taking care' for Axel Griswold," he said aloud, stepping forward into the light. Behind his back he signaled the others to stay in the dimness.

"I remember now—the girl who stamped hands was checking them at the convention entrance when Pete got knocked off the balcony. Were you off on a break? Or off breaking into Steve Tresh's room?" Jupe hoped that Tresh would control his temper. Their only hope was to play for time until Pete and Bob decided to bust in. And what had happened to Rainey up there?

"You were also there at the dinner, breaking up the fight between Tresh and Rottweiler. Did you go out afterward and finish up with Tresh—alone?"

Purvis waggled his head. "You know, I can see why the boss is beginning to get worried about you guys. You've figured out a lot. Too much."

"Not all of it, though. I thought you might have turned out to be the Crimson Phantom, but you don't have the right hands. Too pudgy." They were running out of time. Purvis and his friends were about to make their move.

"Too pudgy, huh?" Purvis said. "You'll find out soon enough—real soon."

Jupe braced himself. "You're awfully sure of the way this will turn out. After all, it's three against three."

Purvis gave them his chipped-tooth smile again. "Yeah, but we make sure we win."

From behind his back he brought out a baseball bat, tapping the fat end into his left hand.

Even though they looked nervous, the two clerks brought up their bats, too.

Then they started down the stairs.

16

Hit and Run

JUPE RAISED HIS FISTS. IT LOOKED LIKE HE WOULD LOSE THIS fight, but he wouldn't take it lying down. If he could take out Purvis, they'd have half a chance. The two clerks obviously hadn't signed on for this. They were just following the head thug.

But tackling Purvis wouldn't be an easy job. He was big, and he handled the bat as if he'd used it before. He advanced confidently down the stairs, the clerks bunched behind him.

Jupe cleared his mind, just as he did at judo practice. He wanted to be open to every nuance of his opponent's movements. His breathing slowed and grew deeper. His hands opened, ready to block or grab.

Purvis and his companions were halfway down the stairs when Jupe spotted two figures in the doorway above.

"Hey, Pete," Jupe called up to them. "The guy in the lead here is the one who punched you out."

Purvis laughed. "I never thought you'd be dumb enough to try that old 'Look behind you!' trick."

While he was talking, Pete and Bob jumped the two clerks. Bob nailed his man with a backhand blow to the side of the head. The guy dropped his bat and slumped onto the steps.

Meanwhile, Pete grabbed his man's bat hand and twisted it up behind him. He plucked the bat from the surprised clerk's grasp and poked down at Purvis with it.

"This is the guy I really want to fight," he said.

Purvis made a quick recovery. With a yell he whipped around, swinging his bat straight at Pete's head. Pete parried the blow awkwardly, and his bat slammed out of his hand. The guy he'd been holding twisted free and began grappling with Bob.

Jupe jumped forward the moment Purvis was distracted. He went up three steps, but his movement alerted the big thug, who swung the bat behind him backhand.

The end of the bat whipped right in front of Jupe's face. Then it cracked into the old wooden railing. Jupe moved up another step, trying to pin the bat with one hand while grabbing for Purvis's wrist with the other.

But Purvis thudded into him with his body, trying to knock Jupe down the stairs. With a grunt of pain Jupe lost his grip. He was forced to cling to the railing to keep from falling. Purvis laughed as he pulled the bat free.

He turned again to swing at Pete and Bob, keeping them back, then went to finish Jupe.

But Jupe wasn't where he was supposed to be. He came in under Purvis's swing. Propelling himself up the staircase like a human missile, his head caught Purvis square in the gut.

Whoof! The thug folded, stumbling back into the arms of Bob and Pete. Even then he kept fighting, catching Bob in the side of the neck with a fist.

"Enough of this," Pete finally said, throwing himself on the guy. They rolled down the stairs together, with Pete landing on top.

He hauled Purvis to his feet and smiled. "You know," he said, "you've got quite a punch. What do you think of mine?"

Then he decked him.

Bob had already taken care of the second clerk. The two Kamikaze employees sat on the steps, all the fight knocked out of them.

"Wow!" Bob called down to Jupe, who was still rubbing his head. "That last move was something. Judo?"

"Stupidity." Jupe winced as his fingers touched a sensitive spot.

"Well, it worked," Pete said happily. "Why were these guys trying to get you, anyway?"

After Jupe brought them up to date, Pete said, "Fine. Do we call the cops now?"

"It's not that easy," Jupe said. "We might get these creeps jailed for assault, but we can't get Griswold."

"Why not?" Pete demanded. "He's a counterfeiter."

"A counterfeiter of *comic books*," Steve Tresh spoke up. "That's not a criminal charge."

"But he's breaking the law!" Pete insisted.

"All they'd be able to get him on is violating some publisher's copyright," Jupe said. "And people usually don't get jailed to keep them around for civil suits like this."

"So he can skip town," DeMento said.

"Maybe even skip the country," Jupe said. "Let's ask some questions and find out just how big this scam is."

One of the scared salesclerks spilled all he knew— about how the comics were printed down in the basement and sold to unsuspecting collectors.

"They probably made a nice profit, too," Tresh said. "Black-and-white comics cost about two grand to counterfeit, and the middle range of collector's items go for about fifty bucks a pop. If they only ran off a hundred of each book, they'd make sixty percent on the deal."

"But Griswold was breaking things up, even getting rid of the press," Jupe pointed out. He looked at one salesclerk. "What was going on?"

"He had another deal going—for color books," the man said.

"Color?" Tresh said. "That costs more like twelve thousand dollars. Where was he getting it done?"

"Taiwan," a voice said from the bottom of the stairs. Purvis, now securely tied up, looked around in disgust. "Axel had some kind of deal with a crooked printer there. The books would be smuggled in as packing material for imported pottery. All of us Kamikaze guys would go into business as distributors up and down the entire coast. It would have been a sweet deal."

"Too bad it's gone sour," Jupe said.

They left the three tied up in the cellar and locked the shop. Rainey was glad to see them. She hadn't enjoyed sitting in the car in such a creepy neighborhood.

"Are you guys okay?" she asked anxiously. "I really got worried when those clerks threw me out and Bob and Pete had to break in."

"We're fine," Jupe assured her, skipping the details. "And now we have to catch Griswold before he gets away."

"How can we stop him?" Pete asked.

"There's still the robbery," Bob suggested. "Maybe we can nail Griswold for that—if we can catch him with the stolen comics."

Rainey sighed. "That sounds like a pretty big if."

◆   ◆   ◆

When they got back to the convention, the bustle and noise came almost as a shock. They had been half-expecting to find the place empty, like Kamikaze Komics.

The girl with the two-toned hair looked very unhappy. She'd been stuck with both entrance jobs— stamping hands and checking admissions. Jupe didn't have the heart to tell her that Purvis wouldn't be back to help her out.

"What now?" Bob asked as they rushed onto the convention floor.

"Find Griswold before he finds us," Pete said. "He sent that gorilla to take care of us. If he sees us scouting around, he'll know something's up."

"I agree," Jupe said. "Find Griswold. And find those comics."

"Hey, what's with you guys?" a booming voice asked. Frank the Crank Carne came barreling through the crowd. "You look excited—all in a sweat. What's up?"

Steve Tresh grabbed him by the arm. "Frank, do you know where Axel Griswold is right now?"

Carne's teeth glistened in a grin behind his beard. "Something exciting *is* up. Is it another disaster old Axel can wring his hands over?"

He laughed, but Jupe got a quick vision of Griswold coming up after the robbery—rubbing his long, thin hands together. Hands that hadn't been stamped, of course. The convention boss wouldn't need an admission ticket, especially with his stooge, Purvis, at the door.

"You know, Griswold's hands match the robber's— long fingers, and no stamp on the back," Jupe said. "I'd think he pulled the job, but two people saw him go into the Gold Room at the time of the robbery." He frowned, thinking.

"I saw him in the Gold Room then. He came in and complained that the projectionist wasn't there," Carne said. "He tried to start the projector, but he couldn't make it work. The stupid thing wasn't even adjusted for the screen. He had to use his bag to prop it up."

"Bag? What bag?" Jupe wanted to know.

Carne shrugged. "He had a canvas bag over his shoulder—like half the people at this convention."

"He didn't have a bag when we met him," Pete said.

"And that wasn't so long before the robbery," Bob added.

"More importantly, what was *in* that bag?" Jupe asked.

"You think it was the costume?" said Rainey.

"Could be." Jupe frowned again. "But the timing is off. How could he get out of the costume and into the Gold Room so quickly?"

"Good question," said Pete.

"I'd like to check out the Gold Room," Jupe announced. "C'mon."

They headed off the convention floor, made a left, and then another left down a long corridor.

"Ever notice how inconvenient they make it to get to these places?" Tresh said with a grin.

Toward the end of the hall, on the right, was the entrance to the Gold Room. Through the closed door they could hear thrilling music and a woman's voice crying, "Blast him, Rock!"

On the left was a blank door without a doorknob. Jupe pushed against it, but the door didn't budge. "Where does this lead?" he asked.

"That's an emergency exit," Carne said. "The convention's on the other side."

Jupe put his ear to the door and caught the sounds of moving bodies and hubbub on the convention floor. "You know," he said, his eyes alight, "this door would have made things very easy for the Crimson Phantom after he pulled the robbery. It's very close to Dan DeMento's stall."

"He'd have to change again," Tresh objected.

"He made his own changing room—the smoke cloud." Jupe turned to Rainey. "Tell me again what you saw when you looked back at the cloud."

She shrugged. "Just a glimpse of red flapping over the guy's shoulder as he disappeared in the smoke."

Jupe nodded. "And which way was he headed?"

Rainey paused. "Gee, I thought it was toward the front door—but it could have been to this side exit instead!"

Jupe grinned. "And the flapping robe could have been Griswold whipping off the costume to stuff it into his bag along with the stolen comics!"

"But I saw him in the Gold Room just before the robbery," Carne began.

"Right," Jupe cut in. "Just before you *heard* about the robbery."

Carne looked confused. "What do you . . . oh. I'm beginning to get what you mean."

"I don't," Pete confessed.

"It would take a couple of minutes for news of the robbery to get out the front door of the convention room and come down this hallway," Bob said.

Jupe nodded. "Right. Just by stepping out the side exit, Griswold could outrun the news and make his appearance in the Gold Room. He'd be safely in there when people started talking about the robbery. No one would suspect him.

"That leaves just one loose end," Jupe added. "The bag Griswold brought into the Gold Room. I wonder if it's still propping up the projector in there."

"We could go find out," Steve Tresh said.

"It would be better if *Griswold* went to find out," Jupe said. "Let's send him a message from the projectionist."

"My pal Hunter is in there now, running the projector," Carne interrupted. "He'll send a message. What do you want him to say?"

Jupe smiled. "How about something like, 'The projector is heating up. There's gonna be a fire!' "

17

Smoking Out a Rat

THE DOORS TO THE GOLD ROOM FLEW OPEN, THROWING A swath of light on the die-hard serial fans. Several didn't even notice—they were fast asleep. Others were too intent on the screen. But a few complained, "Hey! Close that door!"

On the screen Rock Asteroid went into his final struggle with Gung, king of the Muckmen, as thrilling music soared.

The tall figure silhouetted in the door paid no attention to the complaints or the picture. He headed straight for the projector, brushing past Hunter. Grabbing the canvas bag on the table, he started pulling it toward him. The projector shifted to one side, its beam half on, half off the screen.

All that the audience now saw was Rock raising his ray gun. His enemy disappeared.

"What's wrong with the film? What are you doing!" Even the guys who'd been asleep leaped up and began complaining. The shouting got louder when the man yanked the bag out from under the projector. The picture now dropped so the audience could see only the tops of Rock's and Gung's heads. Rock's fish-bowl helmet and Gung's antennae seemed to be dancing as the projector wobbled from side to side.

The yelling drowned out the sound track. It even drowned out the fans shouting, "Quiet! I can't hear."

Seven audience members were silent as they got up and surrounded the man by the projector—the Three Investigators, Madman Dan, Frank the Crank, Steve Tresh, and Rainey Fields. Even with the flickering light the man in the middle was unmistakable—Axel Griswold.

He stood for a moment with the bag clutched in his hands. Then he shrugged and opened it—to take out a tiny ball.

"Hold it!" Jupe shouted, but the ball had already hit the floor.

Dense smoke rose up and Griswold screamed "Fire!"

The real fans didn't even notice. They were busy making Hunter get the picture right—something that got harder and harder as smoke filled the room. Less true-blue fans bolted for the door, jostling Jupe's group apart. Griswold took his chance and charged Rainey, swinging the bag over his head.

She staggered, and he got past her, tearing his way through the still-open doors.

Jupe caught Rainey around the waist, steadying her. "Come on!" he yelled to the others.

They piled through the door to find Griswold

halfway down the hall. He was running full out, brushing people out of his way. As the Investigators plunged after him they saw Griswold straight-arm a fan. The kid went spinning away.

Griswold hit the lobby and kept straight on, jostling past people. He wasn't aiming for the front entrance or the crowd in front of the elevators.

Then Jupe realized. "The stairs! He's going for the fire stairs." Pete took the lead, gaining on Griswold's broken-field run through the lobby crowd.

Griswold skidded around a corner, and they heard the familiar clang of the fire door slamming.

Pete yanked the door open, and then they were all pelting down the stairs to the parking garage. "Go for your cars, not Griswold," Jupe yelled from his place in the middle of the pack. He remembered how DeMento had almost run them down the last time.

Sound strategy. As they came through the door Griswold was already jumping into a bright red Corvette.

The Investigators ran for the Impala. But by the time Pete got it going, the Corvette had whipped through a tight U-turn and was barreling toward the exit ramp. Pete hit the gas and sped after it.

"If this guy gets on the open road, we've had it," he said. "We'll be eating his dust."

But how were they going to stop him? Griswold had a clear path to the ramp.

Then, wheels screaming, DeMento's dark-green

van came careening from behind a pillar. It roared to cut Griswold off.

The Corvette sped up, swerving to avoid DeMento. It nosed its way past, but DeMento's van rammed into the right rear fender.

Griswold fishtailed up the ramp, the crumpled metal on the back of his car screeching.

The green van had a few more dents now. But it lurched through a wide turn up the ramp, staying right on Griswold's tail. Pete and the Investigators now brought up the rear.

Out on Century Boulevard, the Corvette sped up. But it began to shake wildly as it wove through traffic. The Investigators could hear the squeal of tortured rubber. Apparently that fender bender had been more serious than it looked. The dented metal was pressed against the tire.

Griswold couldn't leave them in the dust—too much speed, and he'd lose control of the car. They had a chance!

DeMento stayed behind Griswold, ignoring the protests of the other drivers, keeping the pressure on. Pete started jockeying across the three lanes, trying to get around and cut the Corvette off.

Griswold kept trying to accelerate, but the shaking of his car slowed him down. He just couldn't pull far enough ahead. Several times DeMento thumped into his rear bumper, shaking him up some more.

Even so, they couldn't force him off the road. Griswold kept cutting back and forth, successfully blocking any attempt to pass him. DeMento almost passed him on the left, but Griswold turned into him, putting some dents on the left side of his car.

Cars behind them were blowing their horns, startled by the strange spectacle on the road.

"You know," Bob said, "that Corvette would look more at home in a salvage yard, Jupe."

He was right. Griswold's once magnificent sports car had bashes on both sides, and the bumper had fallen off on one side. Showers of sparks flew as metal screeched against pavement. And that tire was still sending off a shrill protest as it scraped against the ruined fender.

Finally the rubber could stand no more. The tire burst, sending the Corvette veering into the oncoming traffic. Amid the squeal of brakes and a chorus of angry horns, Griswold got control of his machine.

And to his right, Dan DeMento's green van pulled ahead of him, with the Investigators maneuvering to box him in on the left.

Griswold had nothing to lose. His car shuddered wildly as he squeezed between his two pursuers, intending to cross two lanes of traffic and make the next right. DeMento swerved to cut him off.

The Corvette jockeyed for position, coming up dead behind the van.

Then the van's rear doors swung out to reveal Rainey Fields standing in the opening. She looked scared but determined, holding her cape in her hands like a bullfighter. When Griswold tried to swerve past again, she tossed the cape—right onto his windshield.

Griswold missed his turn—but he didn't miss the streetlight just beyond. *Crunch!*

When the cops arrived, they found the pursuers pinning down a groggy but unharmed Griswold. And the bag of loot was still in his hand.

18

Business As Usual

GRISWOLD WAS IN JAIL, ARRESTED FOR THEFT. BUT THE convention had its final day to run. Sunday it was more crowded than ever. The Kamikaze Komics booth was empty, but the other dealers were doing great business.

The crowd was packed around Madman Dan's stall, drawn there by the publicity of his crime-busting exploit. He had extra assistants working behind the tables, and had even been asked for a couple of autographs.

He was engaged in serious business right now, examining a set of comics for sale. "Well, they could be in better condition," he said. "A couple of pages are bent, and this cover is going to come off if you look at it hard. You should have taken better care of them— and not thrown them in my face." He grinned at Jupe.

"It seemed necessary at the time," Jupe said, grinning back. "There was a maiden in distress."

DeMento started counting out twenty-dollar bills. "We agreed on a price if you found the thief," he said, squaring up the pile of money. Then he added more bills. "We'll call this a bonus."

Jupe, Bob, and Pete couldn't believe it. Their investment had paid off handsomely—almost eight hundred bucks!

Jupe put the money in his pocket. "That's really generous of you, Dan."

"Generous, nothing. I'll make it up in fifteen minutes' worth of business," Madman Dan said. "Either that or I'll add it on to the price of *Fan Fun* when it comes back from being evidence. That thing is a *real* collector's item now—the famous phony stolen comic with the famous artist's forged autograph. I may even try to get Steve to sign a real autograph on it."

"Don't push your luck, pal. Be happy I'm signing this other stuff." Steve Tresh was inside the stall, scribbling away with his pen on a stack of comics. "If I autograph that thing, you've got to guarantee me a percentage of the profits."

"These comic people." DeMento sighed. "They all turn into businessmen."

"Except for Frank Carne," Jupe said. "Where is he?"

Tresh laughed. "Where else? In the Gold Room catching another favorite part of *Rock Asteroid*. They finally found something else to hold up the projector."

"Griswold really picked some hiding place," Bob said. "What's going to happen now that his little racket's been exposed?"

"Dealers and collectors from San Diego to Frisco are tearing their hair." DeMento shook his head. "They're not happy to discover that the black-and-whites they bought from Griswold are fakes instead of the bargains they thought they were."

Tresh looked grim. "The scary thing is, he could have kept it up forever if he hadn't gone overboard with that autograph trick. But he went for the bigger money, forging people's signatures onto his phony books to jack up the prices."

"I've heard people moaning about how he took them," Pete said. "He'd show the mark a counterfeit, tell them he'd just picked it up, and ask what they thought about it. They'd discover the autograph, and since Griswold hadn't mentioned *that*, they'd think he hadn't noticed it and snap the book up."

"Their greed was Griswold's gain," Jupe said. "He took a lot of people—even Leo Rottweiler. Then he made his mistake, inviting Steve to the convention—before finding out that Rottweiler had sold his autographed *Fan Fun*."

Tresh nodded. "He figured if I saw the book, it would blow his whole scam."

"Leo sure was in a sweat to buy the book back!" DeMento grinned.

"But you wouldn't sell—so Griswold dressed up as the Crimson Phantom and stole the book," Jupe continued. "That was followed by a campaign to get Tresh out of the convention. Griswold didn't want Steve finding out about the forged autograph. He was afraid his whole operation would start to unravel."

"He didn't know I had other business here," Tresh said.

"And he encouraged Jupe, Pete, and me so he'd look innocent," Bob added. "He figured we'd be easy enough to fool."

"And from our inept start, we sure gave him hope," Jupe admitted. "He planted those comics in Rainey's bag to keep us totally confused."

Pete laughed. "But we nailed him in the end, didn't we?"

"We did—with a lot of help," Jupe said. "Thanks, guys."

"Yeah. Well, if you want to sell the rest of whatever you found in that trunk full of comics, come by the shop someday. I'll see if I can arrange some deals." DeMento waved good-bye.

"Just don't ask for any autographs." Tresh grinned.

The Investigators were headed for the entrance to the hall when they saw camera flashes. There was Rainey Fields, enjoying her new-found celebrity. The media people were all over her—the all-American girl who nabbed a crook superstyle.

"Jupe!" Her face lit up when she saw him.

"Um—hi," he said.

"The silver tongue strikes again," Bob muttered behind him.

Rainey didn't notice. She's looking at me, Jupe realized. *Me!*

"They're busy making me famous, but you're the one who deserves all the credit," she told Jupe. "You figured out who was behind everything, and got out of that jam at the store. You set the trap for Griswold. Know what, Jupe? You're really some kind of guy!"

"I am? I mean, thanks, Rainey." Jupe glanced at the guys behind him and lowered his voice a little. "Maybe after all this is over, we can get together. Where do you live?"

"Um. Portland."

Jupe blinked. "You mean Portland as in Oregon?"

"Yup." Rainey nodded.

"Well, it's a longer drive than I was expecting, but . . ."

"You nut!" Rainey began laughing. "But I hope we *will* get some time to see each other. If I get some modeling jobs in L.A., for instance."

"Or if I get up to Portland." Jupe sighed.

"Don't look *so* sad," Rainey said with a grin. "There's still the convention here. We've got a whole day to enjoy . . ."

Jupe found himself grinning back. "Guys, I'll see you later."

"What about our money?" Pete and Bob wanted to know.

Jupe handed over their shares. "I just found a use for mine," he said with a big smile. "I'm going to spend it on a Rainey day."